Elsie's Impossible Choice

Elsie's Impossible Choice

BOOK TWO

of the
*A Life of Faith:
Elsie Dinsmore*
Series

Based on the beloved books by
Martha Finley

MCP
Mission City Press
Franklin, Tennessee

Book Two of the *A Life of Faith: Elsie Dinsmore* Series

Published by Mission City Press, Inc.

This series is based on the bestselling *Elsie Dinsmore* novels written by Martha Finley and first published in 1868 by Dodd, Mead & Company.

Cover & Interior Design: Richmond & Williams, Nashville, Tennessee
Cover Photography: Michelle Grisco Photography, West Covina, California
Typesetting: BookSetters, White House, Tennessee

Special Thanks to Glen Eyrie Castle and Conference Center, Colorado Springs, Colorado, for Photo Shoot Locations

For more information, write to Mission City Press P.O. Box 681913, Franklin, Tennessee 37068-1913, or visit our Web Site at

www.alifeoffaith.com

Library of Congress Catalog Card Number: 99-65125
Finley, Martha
        Elsie's Impossible Choice
        Book Two of the *A Life of Faith: Elsie Dinsmore* Series
        ISBN 1-928749-02-X

Printed in the United States of America
    4 5 6 7 8 — 05 04 03 02 01

DEDICATION

This book is
dedicated to
the memory of
MARTHA FINLEY

*May the rich legacy of
pure and simple devotion to Christ
that she introduced through
Elsie Dinsmore in 1868
live on in our day and
in generations to come.*

—FOREWORD—

Elsie's Impossible Choice is the second installment in the story of Elsie Dinsmore, a little girl of the Old South who was first introduced to American readers in 1868. Elsie was the creation of Miss Martha Finley (1828-1909), a teacher and Christian writer who eventually produced twenty-eight novels in this series and made "Elsie Dinsmore" a household name in millions of Christian homes in the late 19th and early 20th centuries. In the belief that Elsie's exciting stories have much to say to modern readers, Mission City Press has carefully adapted the original series, preserving the unique style and flavor of Miss Finley's work but updating content and language for 21st century audiences. In spite of the wide gap between Elsie's time and our own, the truths that Elsie learns and lives remain as fresh and inspiring today as when the Elsie novels were first crafted.

Elsie's Impossible Choice continues the story begun in *Elsie's Endless Wait*, the first volume in the *A Life of Faith: Elsie Dinsmore* Series. Elsie is now nine years old and has only recently been joined at the family home by her handsome, young father, Horace Dinsmore, Jr. Although Elsie is both beautiful and intelligent, and the heiress to a large fortune, her life has not been easy. Just a few days after her birth, Elsie lost her mother, and she didn't meet her father until she was eight years old. Raised by a caring housekeeper and her devoted nursemaid, Elsie has nevertheless lacked a loving family and a home of her own. Sent to her grandfather's plantation, Roselands, when she was only four, Elsie was treated as little more than an inconvenient outsider by most of the Dinsmore family. With only her deep love of the Lord to sustain her, Elsie has grown into a kind and thoughtful young girl, determined to live up to her Christian principles every day, in every way.

But Elsie has already come into conflict with her father, particularly over her strict interpretation of God's commandment to "Remember the Sabbath day by keeping it holy." Horace Dinsmore, Jr., though raised in a Christian church, is not a dedicated believer. His daughter, on the other hand, has been taught almost from birth to love God with all her heart and to follow Holy Scripture to the letter. The depth of her faith and commitment was not unusual for a young child of her era. Although America was from the outset populated by people of diverse religious beliefs, many colonists — particularly those who came from England, Scotland, and Ireland — were devout Christians who followed the rigorous Protestant theology of men like John Calvin, John Knox, and John Wesley.

Elsie's earliest and most influential teacher was a woman named Mrs. Murray, a native of Scotland and, like Martha Finley, a Presbyterian. From Mrs. Murray, Elsie would have learned that the Bible is the sole authority for the faithful and that as part of the "priesthood of believers," each person is responsible for upholding the faith. Because Elsie's belief is so firmly grounded in her direct relationship with her Savior, she strongly feels her individual duty to follow His teachings and commandments, no matter what the personal costs. Having accepted God into her heart, Elsie is determined to live according to His ways.

Until her father's return to Roselands, Elsie's faith has not been severely challenged. In fact, the love of her Heavenly Father has given her the support to endure the cold disregard of her family and the unfair treatment she has received at Roselands. But the arrival of Horace Dinsmore, Jr., and Elsie's intense need for the love of her earthly parent may yet threaten her. As Elsie faces her impossible choice, will her beliefs sustain and strengthen her? Will she learn new lessons about love and faith?

～ LIFE AND HEALTH IN ELSIE'S WORLD ～

Life in Elsie's day, even for wealthy families like the Dinsmores, could be hard. Today's readers may find it strange that Elsie and her family are so fearful of illnesses that rarely trouble us, but even a simple cold or fever was life-threatening in Elsie's time. A tiny cut or scratch could lead to a fatal infection. Young people were especially vulnerable because antibiotic medicines and vaccinations against childhood diseases such as diphtheria and measles did not yet exist.

In the 1840s, the United States was still a young country full of farmers and frontierspeople. Sanitation was poor; water was untreated and often contaminated; food was poorly preserved; and disease-carrying rodents plagued cities and farms. In the South, with its hot and humid climate and many wet areas and swamp lands, outbreaks of insect- and water-born diseases such as malaria and yellow fever were common and could claim hundreds or thousands of victims in a very short time.

The people who settled the United States had some advantages — plenty of sunshine and clean air, a variety of fresh foods, and positive attitudes — but illness and disease were constant threats. People of Elsie's time did not understand the relationship between cleanliness and good health: for example, they often drank water from a common cup, spreading contagious diseases rapidly from person to person. Nor did they know about nutrition, vitamins, or the value of a balanced diet, and they often subsisted on meat, bread and sweets. Vitamin and mineral deficiencies led to diseases such as *scurvy*, an exhausting illness that included gum disease and body sores, and *rickets* which resulted in bone deformities in children. Horace Dinsmore, Jr., may not have known nutritional science, but the strict diet he imposed on Elsie was in fact much healthier than the normal fare served at Roselands.

The Dinsmore family was fortunate to have Doctor Barton nearby. Doctor Barton was a trained physician, possibly educated at one of the medical colleges in the North. (The first American medical school was founded in Philadelphia in 1765, but the first Southern medical college was not opened until 1823.)

Many "doctors" however, were no such thing: some communities relied on their apothecary or pharmacist, but rural and frontier areas often depended on the local barber, butcher, teacher, or even preacher who had picked up "doctoring" through observation of primitive folk practices. Our ancestors were also vulnerable to "quacks" (fake healers) and bizarre health theories and treatments.

In the 19th century, doctors were few and far between in the countryside, and even the best physicians knew very little about the causes of and cures for most diseases. They did not know about bacteria and viruses or the importance of sterile, germ-free surgery and antiseptics to clean wounds. Because their knowledge of medical science was so limited, doctors could do little more than treat the obvious symptoms of illness, and their treatments were often worse than their cures. For instance, they believed that the best cure for a fever was to keep the patient warm under heavy blankets; they confined bed-ridden patients to dark, closed rooms in the belief that light and fresh air were harmful. *Phlebotomy* or bleeding — taking amounts of the patient's blood over a period of time in an attempt to remove the "bad blood" that was believed to cause illness — was a routine treatment even for minor medical problems. (Today, we know that cooling a patient reduces fever, that light and fresh air often promote healing, and that taking blood only saps a patient's strength, reduces the body's natural ability to fight infections, and can cause anemia or death.)

Doctors relied on medications made from plants, herbs, and other natural elements. The early settlers learned many helpful cures from the Native Americans. Some of these tribal remedies — such as chewing willow bark for headaches and slippery elm bark for upset stomachs — are still valid today.

But other so-called "cures" were based on nothing more than myth and superstition. Victims of *tuberculosis* (a wasting disease that attacks the body's tissues) were advised to drink milk from cows that grazed in a churchyard, although we now know that unpasteurized milk can actually contain tuberculosis and other disease bacteria. (It was not until late in the 19th century that French scientist Louis Pasteur discovered heating to destroy bacteria in milk, a process that is called "pasteurization" in his honor.) Medicines were concocted of whatever was available including harmful, toxic elements such as mercury.

Although we aren't told the exact nature of the illnesses that affect the Dinsmores and their friends, it is possible to make educated guesses. Elsie's mother died shortly after Elsie was born, probably from complications of childbirth. Even into the 20th century, childbirth was extremely dangerous, and countless young mothers and their infants did not survive it. Elsie's friend Herbert Carrington suffers from a hip disease which may have been tuberculosis but was more likely *polio*, which causes paralysis. If a polio victim survived, he was likely to be crippled and ill for life.

When people in Elsie's time were stricken with high fever, chills and other symptoms, they were said to have the "ague." This was an all-purpose term that covered illnesses ranging from influenza to malaria and cholera. A related term was "brain fever" which was frequently used to explain undiagnosed illness in children. *Pneumonia* often resulted from other, less serious illnesses. Injuries to the limbs — such as sprains and simple breaks — required careful attention. If such a wound was complicated or became infected, doctors had no choice except amputation.

So in Elsie's world, the possibly of disease and death were daily realities for everyone, young and old. With few educated doctors, no modern hospitals or public health services, no trained and caring nurses, and very little knowledge of how to treat illness and injuries, it is little wonder many people believed that good health or bad health was a sign of God's judgment. It was not until near the end of the 19th century that Americans began to understand the origins of illness and to realize that changes in their environment and behavior — pure water and sanitation, healthy eating, cleanliness at home and work — could affect their health and well-being. But for a child of Elsie's generation, life truly was a precious gift that could be lost at any moment.

DINSMORE FAMILY TREE

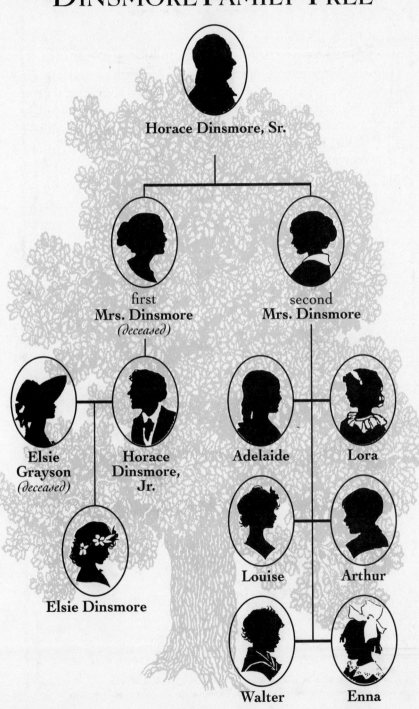

Horace Dinsmore, Sr.

first
Mrs. Dinsmore
(deceased)

second
Mrs. Dinsmore

Elsie
Grayson
(deceased)

Horace
Dinsmore,
Jr.

Adelaide

Lora

Elsie Dinsmore

Louise

Arthur

Walter

Enna

SETTING

*R*oselands, a large plantation near a coastal city in the Old South in the early 1840s, some years before the American Civil War and the abolition of slavery.

CHARACTERS

The Dinsmores of Roselands Plantation

Mr. Horace Dinsmore, Sr. — The owner and master of Roselands; Elsie's grandfather.

Mrs. Dinsmore — Mr. Dinsmore's second wife and mother of six children:

Adelaide — Age 17	**Lora** — Age 15
Louise — Age 13	**Arthur** — Age 11
Walter — Age 9	**Enna** — Age 7

Mr. Horace Dinsmore, Jr. — The only son of Horace Dinsmore, Sr., and his first wife. Once married to Elsie Grayson of New Orleans, Horace has recently returned to Roselands after an absence of more than eight years.

Elsie Dinsmore — Age 9; the daughter of Horace Dinsmore, Jr., and Elsie Grayson, who died shortly after Elsie's birth. Born in New Orleans, Elsie has lived at Roselands since she was four years old.

Miss Day — The children's teacher.

Mrs. Murray — A Scots Presbyterian woman of deep Christian faith. One of Elsie's earliest companions, she is now living in her native Scotland.

Mrs. Brown — The housekeeper at Roselands.

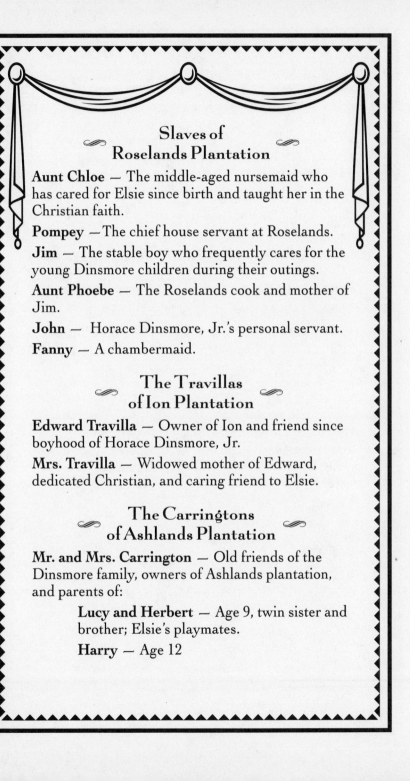

Slaves of
Roselands Plantation

Aunt Chloe — The middle-aged nursemaid who has cared for Elsie since birth and taught her in the Christian faith.

Pompey — The chief house servant at Roselands.

Jim — The stable boy who frequently cares for the young Dinsmore children during their outings.

Aunt Phoebe — The Roselands cook and mother of Jim.

John — Horace Dinsmore, Jr.'s personal servant.

Fanny — A chambermaid.

The Travillas
of Ion Plantation

Edward Travilla — Owner of Ion and friend since boyhood of Horace Dinsmore, Jr.

Mrs. Travilla — Widowed mother of Edward, dedicated Christian, and caring friend to Elsie.

The Carringtons
of Ashlands Plantation

Mr. and Mrs. Carrington — Old friends of the Dinsmore family, owners of Ashlands plantation, and parents of:

> **Lucy and Herbert** — Age 9, twin sister and brother; Elsie's playmates.
>
> **Harry** — Age 12

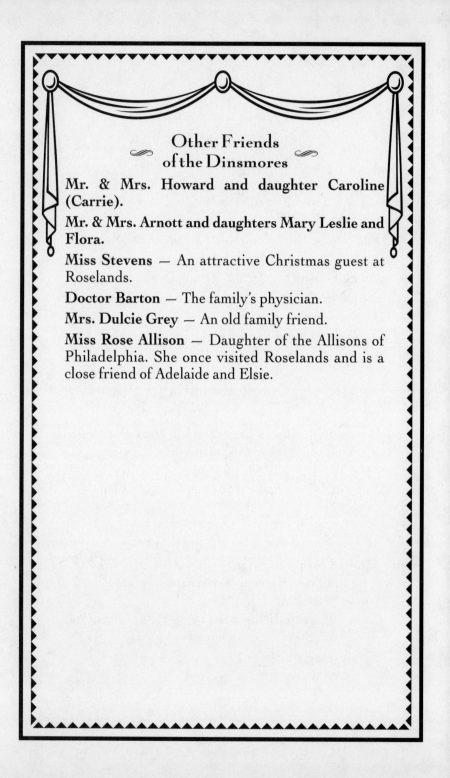

Other Friends
of the Dinsmores

Mr. & Mrs. Howard and daughter Caroline (Carrie).

Mr. & Mrs. Arnott and daughters Mary Leslie and Flora.

Miss Stevens — An attractive Christmas guest at Roselands.

Doctor Barton — The family's physician.

Mrs. Dulcie Grey — An old family friend.

Miss Rose Allison — Daughter of the Allisons of Philadelphia. She once visited Roselands and is a close friend of Adelaide and Elsie.

CHAPTER

1

Changes in the Air

*"There is a time for everything,
and a season for every
activity under
heaven."*

ECCLESIASTES 3:1

It was one of those clear, late fall days in the South when the sky turns a bright, pure blue and the air is crisp and cool. As was her habit, Elsie Dinsmore had awakened early. While her nursemaid, Aunt Chloe, bustled to build a warming fire in the grate, Elsie wrapped herself in a soft quilt and tiptoed to the window. What she saw was like a picture from one of her favorite fairy tale books.

The garden of Roselands, still alive with colorful blooms and deep green shrubbery, appeared to have been sprinkled with diamonds during the night. A light coating of frost made everything sparkle brilliantly in the early morning sunlight. Farther away, in the paddock, a half-dozen of the family's saddle horses pawed at the air and pranced in nervous excitement. They, too, seemed to radiate light as a faint mist rose from their sleek coats. Even the fields and the hills in the distance were touched with the magic.

Elsie herself felt strangely excited. At supper the night before, she had heard her grandfather tell her father that a change was in the air. Was this what he meant, she wondered. She certainly felt as if something were going to happen. It was like the feeling she had just before a birthday.

The frost had disappeared by the time Elsie was dressed. As she did each morning, she settled into her little, rosewood rocking chair — so prized because it was a gift from her father — to read her Bible and talk to Jesus, her beloved Savior and Friend. She enjoyed this time with the Lord immensely. She began by asking the Lord to open her heart and mind to the Scriptures; then she read and reflected on a passage and memorized a verse from the passage she had read. Finally, she knelt to say her morning prayers and asked the Lord to grant her the "fruit of the spirit" of which Paul spoke in the fifth chapter of the Book of Galatians — "love, joy, peace, patience, kindness, goodness, faithfulness, gentleness and self-control."

Resuming her seat, she took up her geography book, intending to memorize the day's lesson before the breakfast bell was rung. But her thoughts kept drifting away.

"What troubles your young brain on this beautiful morning, birdie?" came a cheerful voice from behind her. "Or do you always read your books bottom-to-top?"

"Oh, Aunt Adelaide!" Elsie said, flushing brightly as she looked first into her aunt's smiling face and then at the book in her own hands. Indeed it was turned upside down so that the map on the page seemed to be tumbling headlong into her lap.

"You were daydreaming," Adelaide said with a smile.

Laughing at herself now, Elsie replied, "I guess I was. I was thinking about Christmas. It's coming soon, and I don't know what I can give to Papa. I was thinking about bedroom slippers, but he has such a handsome pair. And I've already made a purse for him. Besides, I want to give him a present better than slippers or a purse. Can you help me chose something special for him, dear Auntie?"

"I shall have to put my thinking cap on," Adelaide said. She scrunched her face into a comically serious look and made a gesture as if tugging something down tight upon her head. She pulled at her chin as she paced toward Elsie's bed, then back again to stand over her niece, who was greatly enjoying this show.

"I have it!" Adelaide exclaimed suddenly. "I know just what would please your father more than anything else you could give him." She dropped to her knees at Elsie's side and cupped the little girl's chin in her hand. "Your portrait, my dear. He would love to have a miniature portrait of his own daughter's beautiful face."

Elsie's bright hazel eyes rounded with pleasure. "Oh, yes! What a good idea. But — but how can I get it done without his knowing? It must be a surprise for him."

"You leave that to me," Adelaide said with confidence. "I'll manage the arrangements, but you must count your money to see how much you can spend."

At that moment, they heard the ringing of the bell from downstairs. Adelaide rose, smoothing her billowing skirt. She took Elsie's hand and looked down into the girl's beaming face. "You will give away our secret with that big smile of yours," Adelaide warned, "so put on your everyday face. That's better. Now, let's go to the table. I find I'm quite hungry after so much hard work."

As Elsie struggled to control her excitement, they walked hand-in-hand from the room.

Adelaide thought a great deal of Elsie as she went about her duties that day — and not just in connection with the Christmas gift. There had been such a change in the child in the past few months.

Adelaide remembered five years before, when Elsie had first arrived at Roselands, a shy four-year-old with only her nursemaid and an old Scottish housekeeper for her companions. Adelaide's father, the senior Mr. Horace Dinsmore, had taken the child in because he had little other choice. Elsie was his only grandchild, the daughter of his son's rash marriage to a wealthy — but in Mr. Dinsmore's mind, socially unsuitable — girl from New Orleans. Mr. Dinsmore and the girl's guardian had managed to separate the young couple when the marriage was just a few months old, and young Horace Dinsmore had been sent off to college and then to Europe. The young wife had died soon after Elsie's birth (from a broken heart, to Adelaide's way of thinking), and the baby was raised in the home of her guardian. But when the guardian died, there had been nowhere for Elsie to go but to the Dinsmores and their plantation, Roselands.

Adelaide, who was the eldest of old Mr. Dinsmore's children with his second wife, had paid little attention to Elsie at first. She had assumed the child would simply fit in with her own five young brothers and sisters. But Elsie was not like any of them. She had been raised in the strict Christian faith of Mrs. Murray, the guardian's housekeeper, and Aunt Chloe, her loving nursemaid. Even as a small girl, Elsie had displayed a measure of simplicity, honesty, and sweetness that was, Adelaide had to admit, at odds with the rest of the family. Mr. Dinsmore, Sr., was often annoyed with Elsie because of what he said was her lack of spunk. "Why won't that girl ever stand up for herself?" he would demand. "It's hard to believe she's a Dinsmore," he'd say in disgust.

Adelaide's mother, who was Elsie's step-grandmother, had taken an instant dislike to the child and shown her not even the common courtesy she would give a stranger. Adelaide knew that her mother was deeply jealous of Elsie. The elder Mrs. Dinsmore envied the little girl's inherited wealth and obvious beauty. She feared that someday Elsie would overshadow her own daughters — Adelaide and her sisters Lora, Louise, and Enna. Adelaide hated to think ill of her own mother, but she had come to understand that many of Elsie's troubles were the fruits of Mrs. Dinsmore's jealousy and bad temper.

Adelaide had a harder time understanding her half-brother, Horace, Jr. He was the child's father, but had never laid eyes on Elsie until a year before. He had stayed in Europe until Elsie was more than eight years old, and when he finally returned to Roselands, he had been strangely cold and distant with his daughter. It had been a sad time, and Elsie suffered greatly. Adelaide had sometimes tried to intervene on Elsie's behalf, and so had Horace's best friend, Edward Travilla. But it had taken a terrible accident — one that came close to costing Elsie her life — to bring the young father and his adoring daughter together.

The change in both was remarkable. Horace was now devoted to his little girl, protecting her in every way. And Elsie's natural character had blossomed. Oh, she was as generous and sweet-natured as ever, but now she was lively and no longer so shy. Given her father's love, Elsie had become a rosy, laughing girl.

There was still one issue, however. Whatever sorrow or joy came her way, Elsie's Christian faith was unshakable, and Adelaide worried that Horace, who took such pride in being an upright man of reason and moral sense, might never understand Elsie's personal devotion to God. If Adelaide envied her niece anything, it was this deep and abiding faith and the strength it seemed to give Elsie even in the darkest moments.

"Oh, well," Adelaide told herself, "it's no good begging trouble. Elsie and Horace are as happy as can be. What could possibly come between them now?" With her needle, she tucked a silken thread into the monogram she was embroidering on a linen handkerchief and neatly clipped the thread with her scissors. She carefully folded the work and stored it in her sewing basket. "It's time I find Elsie and tell her the good news."

Elsie was in her room. She had just returned from her afternoon pony ride, and Aunt Chloe was busy changing her from her riding outfit into a pretty dress when her aunt entered.

"I have it all arranged," Adelaide said. "I have just learned that your father is going away on a business trip and he will be gone for two weeks. Unless he should take it into his head to carry you with him, that will give us just enough time to have your portrait painted, and your Papa won't suspect a thing."

Instead of the expected smile, Adelaide found herself gazing at a little face full of dismay. "What is the matter, dear?" she asked. "I thought you would be delighted that it has worked out so well. But you look as if you just lost your closest friend."

"But, Aunt Adelaide," Elsie began, a little quiver in her voice. "Two whole weeks without Papa? He's never been away for so long since he came home to us."

"Oh, pooh! The time will pass before you know it, won't it, Aunt Chloe?"

"Yes ma'am," Chloe agreed, "just so long as this child has something to occupy her while her Papa is away."

"You see, Elsie," Adelaide went on reassuringly. "You and I will be very busy while your father is away. Now, how much money do you have?"

"I've saved two months' allowance. That's twenty dollars. Will it be enough?"

"Not quite, I'm afraid, but I will lend you the difference."

"Thank you, Auntie," Elsie replied, but her little brow furrowed. "You are so kind, but Papa has expressly told me never to borrow from anyone or run into debt in any way."

A quick, impatient thought passed through Adelaide's mind about Horace's absurdly strict rules for Elsie, but she said pleasantly, "Well, never mind. We will manage it somehow. And you shall have a wonderful surprise for your father."

Elsie did not have a chance to be alone with her father until after supper that night. Horace had noticed that she seemed more quiet than usual at the evening meal, and when they adjourned to the library, he asked if she were feeling well.

"Yes, Papa, but —" Tears welled in her eyes, and the words caught in her throat.

"What troubles you, Daughter?" he asked with concern, for Elsie had cried so little of late that he knew something was wrong.

"Oh, Papa, are you really going away?"

Horace was relieved, and a little flattered, too. "Yes, darling, I must go to New Orleans on some business regarding your property there. I considered having you come with me, but I decided not to take you away from your studies so near the Christmas holiday. I will reconsider, however, if you want me to."

Elsie thought carefully. Of course she wanted to be with her father, but this would also be her only chance to secure his Christmas present. "I always want to be where you are, Papa," she said at last, "but you know what is best for me. I'll miss you very much."

Elsie's Impossible Choice

"No more than I will miss you, but I really think it's best for you to stay home this time."

"When are you leaving, Papa?"

"Tomorrow afternoon, just after dinner." He saw the worried look on her face and hugged her close. "Remember, Elsie, that the sooner I go, the sooner I will return. Two weeks may seem like a very long time to you, but I think you'll be surprised how quickly it passes. What do you say if I write you a letter every day?"

Elsie brightened immediately. "That would be so good of you, Papa. I love to get letters, and I have never had a letter from you."

"Then it's settled. And for being an understanding daughter, I have something for you." Horace reached into his coat and withdrew his purse. "I believe you may have use for a little extra pocket money for buying Christmas presents. Do you think you can use this?" He took a fifty-dollar note from the purse and placed it in her hand.

"Oh, thank you, Papa!" she cried with amazement. "I've never had *half* so much before. May I spend it all?"

"Provided you don't waste it," Horace answered with a smile. "And you must keep a strict accounting of every penny you spend."

A look of concern clouded Elsie's eyes. "But must I tell you *every*thing I buy?"

"Yes, you must, but not until after Christmas, if you'd rather not."

"Thank you, Papa. I'll keep my account carefully, and you can see it after Christmas."

Changes in the Air

Though Elsie could not help crying when her father's carriage disappeared down the driveway the next day, the two weeks did go by much faster than she had imagined possible.

The morning after his departure, when the rest of the family was gathered at breakfast, Pompey, who was chief among the house servants, brought in the day's mail. Her grandfather, slowly sorting through the large stack of correspondence, finally announced, "Two for Elsie! Let's see here — one is from her father and the other from Miss Rose Allison, I believe." Elsie could hardly restrain herself as Mr. Dinsmore turned the two envelopes this way and that, examining the addresses and postmarks. Finally he handed the letters to her, saying, "If you have done with your breakfast, you'd better run along and read them."

"Oh, thank you, Grandpa!" Elsie almost sang out.

"Whose letter do you think she will read first?" asked Lora, the second of the Dinsmores' four daughters, when Elsie had left the room.

"Her father's, of course," Adelaide said knowingly. "She loves Rose Allison dearly, but her father means more to her than all the rest of the world put together."

"That is a matter of small concern to the rest of the world," remarked Mrs. Dinsmore with an unpleasant snort.

Adelaide's reply was quiet but direct: "You are probably right, Mamma. But still, there are *some* who prize Elsie's affection most highly."

The letters continued to arrive each day, just as Horace had promised, until the final letter came, telling of his imminent return. Elsie was so excited by this news that she skipped out of her room and into the hallway, nearly colliding with Mrs. Dinsmore.

11

"What are you doing, running about in this mad fashion?" the irritated woman demanded. "Will you never learn to act like a lady?"

"I will try, ma'am," Elsie said softly, lowering her head so that Mrs. Dinsmore could not see the happy smile that still played on her mouth. "I am just so glad that Papa is coming home today."

"That's hardly an excuse," Mrs. Dinsmore complained sourly, and with a toss of her head, she moved on. But not even she could dampen the little girl's anticipation on this day.

Elsie could hardly eat anything at dinner, and as soon as she was excused, she took her station at one of the drawing room windows that offered a full view of the wide driveway that ran from the road to the house. At last she saw it, a distant cloud of dust that signaled the arrival of a carriage. She rushed to put on a light coat, for the evening came early now and there was a cool breeze blowing, and she reached the portico steps just as the carriage pulled up. The instant the carriage stopped, she ran forward to be caught up in her father's arms.

"How good it is to be home with you again," Horace declared, hugging her close.

Elsie kissed his cheek. "Papa, you're so cold," she said. "There's a fire in the drawing room."

"Is there one in my room?" he asked.

"Yes, Papa," she answered, smiling, for she had made sure that her father's room was warm and well prepared for his return.

"Then go upstairs, and we shall see what I have brought back from my trip."

Elsie went into the house while Horace directed his servant, John, to see that several heavy trunks were conveyed upstairs. In his room, as they waited for the luggage to be delivered, Horace changed from his heavy traveling coat and boots into the dressing gown and slippers that Elsie had carefully laid out for him, and she told him most — but not all — of what she had done during his absence.

"Have your school lessons gone well?" he asked.

"I believe so, Papa. I tried very hard, but you will get my report from Miss Day."

"No, Elsie, I trust your own report to be truthful," he said, and she blushed with pleasure, for there had been a time, not long before, when he had unfairly suspected her of a falsehood.

"Besides," Horace went on, "I understand that your governess has gone to her home in the North until the New Year and you are now on holiday. I think you've earned a vacation from school, and I will allow you to play almost all the time. But to keep your mind sharp, I may give you a lesson now and then. What do you think?"

Elsie was delighted because she always enjoyed learning from her father; Horace taught her in subjects like geology and botany that were not included in the schoolroom.

"Yes, please do, Papa," she said.

"Well, then, we can spend an hour on study every morning. But aren't you expecting some company?"

"Oh, there will be a house full," Elsie said seriously. "The Howards, the Arnotts, and all the Carringtons are coming, and some others, I believe. But, Papa, when there are so many visitors and they stay for so long, sometimes they disagree, and it's not so much fun. I think I'll especially enjoy having an hour alone with you while they are here."

Horace laughed out loud and ruffled his child's thick, brown curls; he, too, could grow quite weary of a house filled with guests. "Well," he asked with a twinkle, "when are your little friends coming?"

"Tomorrow is the Sabbath, so they will be here on Monday, I think."

A tap at the door interrupted their conversation, and John put his head in to ask, "Should I brings these trunks in now, sir?" Horace agreed and handed John a heavy ring of keys. When the luggage was arrayed on the floor and the lids unlocked and raised, Horace said, "Thank you, John. Don't worry about the unpacking now. I think my daughter can help with that."

Smiling, Horace pointed at one of the cases. "Try that hatbox, Elsie, dear."

Elsie lifted the cover of the large, round box and took out a lovely, dark green velvet hat trimmed with two small ostrich feathers. "It's so pretty, Papa!" she exclaimed.

"Then let's try it on you. There. It fits just right, and it is very becoming to you. The color in those feathers brings out the green in your eyes."

There was much more for Elsie to find — several handsome dresses made of the softest merino wool, three beautiful silk dresses in the latest fashion for young girls, and a luxurious, fur-trimmed, velvet pelisse coat that matched her new hat.

Horace selected one of the dresses and said, "We must see if these fit. All the dresses are cut from the same pattern, so take this one to Aunt Chloe and have her help you into it. Then come back and let me see the results."

A few minutes later, Elsie danced back into his room. The golden silk brocade dress fit her perfectly, and Horace could not help smiling. His child was lovely, and every day she seemed to grow more like her beautiful mother. Elsie twirled with pleasure, and Horace said, "It's a perfect fit.

You can tell Aunt Chloe to dress you in it for church tomorrow, and if the weather is still cool, you can wear your new coat and hat as well."

Elsie suddenly stopped her dance and looked at him seriously. "But Papa, I'm afraid that I shall be thinking only about my new clothes if I wear them on the Sabbath."

"That's nonsense, Elsie," he said with a hint of irritation. "Sunday is a day much like any other, and this sensitivity of yours about the Sabbath displeases me very much, as you know. Now, don't look so distressed. I'm sure you will get over it by-and-by. In fact, I believe I have seen improvements in your attitude already."

Their last confrontation had been caused by Elsie's strict beliefs about observing the Sabbath, but he was determined not to make a problem of it this time. It was an indication of how little Horace understood of Elsie's faith that he mistook her obedience to the Scriptures for childishness.

But what he said had frightened Elsie. Her father turned to remove some other things from one of his trunks and did not see the anguish in her face. Was he right, she asked herself. Had she indeed changed? Was she less conscientious in her attention to God's commands? Had she dishonored her Savior? Beyond her control, a sharp cry escaped her lips as she lifted a fervent prayer to her ever-forgiving Savior and Friend.

At the sound, Horace turned to her in astonishment. "What is it, my child?" he asked and drew her to him. "Is it what I said? I surely didn't mean to hurt your feelings over such a trifling matter."

Elsie couldn't stop her tears now, and she clung to her father as she sobbed out her doubts. "Oh, Papa. Can it be true that I don't love Jesus as I used to?"

Elsie's Impossible Choice

"Is that all, dear? Well, I think you are a very good girl, though you are being a bit silly perhaps."

He wiped her tears with his handkerchief and changed the subject, cheering her with his tales of what he had seen and done in New Orleans. Still, she was more reserved than she had been for some time, and after she had gone to dress for supper, Horace thought about the strange incident. "I wonder if I will ever understand her," he said aloud to himself. "It's strange how often I seem to hurt her when I mean only to please."

But that night, Elsie took her questions to the One who always listens. She asked Him to guard her heart against anything that might take first place from Him, and she once again felt the peace that comes from knowledge of His tender love.

The next morning, Horace could not find even a trace of sadness about his child. Elsie wore her new clothes to church without complaint. In truth, she was not even conscious of the handsome new garments, devoting her full attention to the services.

After the family's Sunday dinner, Horace gave Elsie permission to join him as he read in the library. Elsie, who believed that it was only permissible to read the Bible or other praiseworthy words on the Sabbath, brought her own book.

After she had gone through several pages, she asked, "Did you ever read *Pilgrim's Progress*, Papa?"

"Yes, I read it when I was a boy, but I have nearly forgotten it now. Do you enjoy it?"

16

"Oh, yes, I do. I think it the best book I have ever read next to the Bible."

"But as I recall now, isn't it a rather foolish story about a man with some great load on his back?" Horace asked with a smile.

"You're teasing me, Papa. I think it's a wonderful story, not foolish at all. It's about a man named Christian who struggles with his burden of sins. It's only when he looks to Jesus and trusts in His work on the Cross that his load of sin is lifted. And it's true, Papa! I have felt it myself."

Horace was not sure how to reply. Elsie's understanding of spiritual matters always surprised him, and he worried that Elsie was too serious about such ideas. Because he had never personally experienced the healing and comfort of God's forgiving love, he supposed that his child's habit of thinking would make her unhappy and somber; more than anything now, Horace wanted to spare Elsie from any kind of unhappiness.

"Frankly, Elsie," he said, "I'm inclined to object to your reading such dismal things."

"It's not dismal at all, Papa!" Elsie exclaimed. "It's about *wonderful* news, for the Bible tells us that 'as far as the east is from the west, so far has He removed our transgressions from us.' We simply have to trust in Jesus."

"You are too young for preaching, Elsie," Horace replied gently. "Now, go back to your book, and we'll talk later."

But Horace was vaguely troubled by Elsie's words, and it was some minutes before he could resume his own reading.

After supper that evening, the house was unusually quiet. There were none of the business visitors who so often came at night, and the other Dinsmores were each preparing for their holiday guests. Elsie went to her father's room, and as had become their custom on Sunday nights, they read several chapters of the Bible together, and Elsie sang some of her favorite hymns, with Horace joining in when the words were familiar to him.

"This has been such a nice evening, Papa, like the times I had when Miss Allison was here, only —" She hesitated.

"Only what, Elsie? You can tell me."

She finally said, "It's only that I wish you would pray with me, Papa, as Miss Rose always did."

Her words pricked both his conscience and his heart, but Horace tried to keep his tone lighthearted: "I fear that I never learned how, Daughter, so I think you will have to do all the praying for both of us."

And Elsie did pray that night, when she was alone. Her prayer was not for herself, however, but for her dear Papa, that he might learn to love Jesus and accept the gift of God's perfect love. Her father, she knew, was always careful to observe the outward forms of religion, but her deepest wish was that he would one day truly open his heart to her precious Redeemer.

CHAPTER 2

Holiday Surprises

*"Every good and perfect gift is from
above, coming down from the
Father of the heavenly lights,
who does not change like
shifting shadows."*

JAMES 1:17

*E*lsie woke early on Monday morning. It was only two days before Christmas, and soon her friends would begin arriving at Roselands. She wanted to be up and ready, but Aunt Chloe directed her to stay in bed until the fire was going and the room was toasty.

"You aren't going to miss a thing, child, by keeping to that bed a while longer. Breakfast's going to be late anyhow," Chloe informed her, "because Mrs. Dinsmore wants the family to sleep late today if they like. But your Papa told me to have you ready for your walk with him as usual. And he wants you to have this milk and crackers," she gestured to a small tray on the dresser, "so your stomach won't be grumbling."

By the time Elsie had her devotional time, been dressed, and eaten her snack, the house was just beginning to stir. At half past seven precisely, she tapped at her father's door. Horace, always an early riser whatever the season, was ready for their morning walk. After making sure that Elsie was warmly wrapped, he took her hand, and they went outside.

The cold air struck her and painted her cheeks a bright pink. "It's going to be such a happy day, isn't it, Papa?" she asked.

"Yes, my child, and I wish I could make every day happy for you," Horace replied. "But it cannot always be so in this life."

"That's in the Bible," Elsie said earnestly. "It says 'In this world you will have trouble . . .' But I'm not frightened, Papa, because the Bible also says that Jesus loves me and

He will never leave me or forsake me. He will never let anything happen except what is good for me. Oh, Papa, it's such a happy thing to have the dear Lord Jesus for your friend! I do love Him so."

Elsie looked up at her father, but he seemed deep in thought, so she fell silent. In fact, Horace was considering again how everything seemed to bring Elsie to her love of Jesus. "She loves Him better than me," he thought with a little stab of pain. "She has told me so often enough. Yet how much I want to be everything to her, as she is to me now. Still, I doubt that many daughters love their fathers so well." He gave Elsie's hand a gentle squeeze.

Elsie responded as if she had read his mind. "And next to Jesus, I love you, Papa. I love you better than anything in the world."

The day's activities began normally enough. After breakfast, Elsie practiced at the piano for an hour, then she joined her father for their hour of lessons. He took her out again for her daily horseback ride — it was important to Horace that his daughter should be an experienced horsewoman — but when they returned, the guests had indeed begun to arrive.

Elsie was thrilled to see Caroline Howard, one of her favorite friends, and after greeting all the adults, the two little girls quickly slipped away to Elsie's room. They had so much to talk about, especially Carrie's long visit to the North, where she had attended school for a year, and the return of Elsie's beloved Papa. Their tongues ran very fast as they giggled and gabbed.

"Elsie, I believe your beautiful hair is more curly than ever," Carrie said as she playfully tossed one of her friend's ringlets. "I say, could you possibly let me have one of your curls? I could have it made into a braided bracelet for my Mamma's Christmas present. They are so fashionable now, but my own hair is just too thin and straight."

Elsie, who thought Carrie's long blonde hair to be quite lovely, nevertheless agreed. "But be careful to cut a curl that won't be missed," she warned as Caroline took the sewing scissors to the back of Elsie's head. She heard a little snip.

"Don't worry," Carrie laughed as she held up a long, bouncing ringlet. "You have so many curls, it will never be missed."

"But how can you get a bracelet made in time?" Elsie asked. "Christmas is the day after tomorrow." Then she had an idea: "I know. Perhaps Papa will take us to town this afternoon, and you can go to the shop. Let's go and ask him now."

It was almost dinner time, and all the adults were gathered in the drawing room. The room seemed to buzz with the sounds of talk and laughter, as it always does when old friends gather after long absences. The air was rich with the scent of pine from the branches and wreaths with which Adelaide and her sisters had decorated all the rooms of Roselands. Elsie's father was talking to a gentleman whom Elsie did not know, so she and Carrie waited patiently until Horace noticed them. "What is it, Elsie?" he asked at last.

"Papa, Carrie and I want to go into town today to finish our Christmas shopping. Will you take us, please?"

"I'm sorry, dear, but I have a business appointment this afternoon that I cannot break. But I'll gladly take you both tomorrow, if the Howards agree."

Elsie's Impossible Choice

Elsie, carried away with the excitement of her plan, went on, "Then can we have one of the carriages and get Pompey or Ajax to drive us?"

"I'm afraid that you and Carrie are much too young to go to town alone. Just wait until tomorrow when I can take you."

Forgetting herself, Elsie tried once more. She took her father's hand in hers, and both her voice and her eyes were full of coaxing. "But, Papa, we want to go today," she whined. "Please say yes. We will be very good on our own. Oh, please let us go, Papa!"

Horace drew away his hand and spoke sternly. "You know that when I say no, that is exactly what I mean, Elsie."

Elsie hung her head, for she knew it was useless to ask again. Coaxing never worked with him, and she was a little ashamed to have tried.

Adelaide, who was standing nearby, had overheard the conversation. She stepped to Horace's side, saying, "Perhaps I can help, Brother. I intend to go to town myself this afternoon. Will you allow the girls to come with me?"

"Well, that will be fine," Horace said, for he was not truly angry with his daughter. "Elsie and Carrie, run along now, and get Mrs. Howard's permission for your trip. You should be ready to go right after dinner."

The afternoon's shopping was great fun. Adelaide was a good companion, and they found the shop where braided bracelets were made. The shopkeeper was not sure that the work could be completed in time, but he promised Carrie that he would try. Elsie used the last of her money to purchase gifts for each of the house servants, and Adelaide completed her gift buying. Their last stop was to pick up the package that contained Elsie's gift for her

24

father. It was growing dark when the carriage finally arrived back at Roselands, and Horace was waiting on the steps for them.

When he caught sight of Elsie's large stack of boxes and bags, he laughed. "You seem to have bought something for everyone. Is there a package for me in all those bundles?"

"I'm sorry, Papa. There's none for you," Elsie replied, trying very hard not to laugh. (It was quite true, too, for Elsie had entrusted Horace's gift to her aunt.)

"Then I shall claim my present now," Horace said. He picked Elsie up and swung her over his shoulder like a rag doll. Everyone was laughing now, and with Carrie Howard running ahead of them, they all went into the warm, brightly lit house.

Because there were so many guests at Roselands, the young people were to have their meals in the playroom during the holidays. It was a merry group that gathered for supper, with the Dinsmore children — Lora and Louise, their younger brothers, Arthur and Walter, and the "baby" of the family, Enna — and their friends. Elsie was delighted to see Mary Leslie Arnott and her little sister, Flora. Mary Leslie was a fun-loving girl, about Elsie's age, and she always made the other children laugh.

The housekeeper at Roselands, Mrs. Brown, presided over the children's table, seeing that each young person was well fed and that manners were attended to.

After their meal, the children decided to play some games, and they were soon joined by Elsie's father. Although most had never met Horace before — and some were quite shy in his presence — they soon discovered that he was more than amiable and ready to enter into their play. By the end of the evening, Horace had made himself very popular with Elsie's friends, and she was so proud of him. She had no idea of how quickly the evening was passing until she heard the clock chime on the half-hour and felt her father's hand on her shoulder.

"It's bedtime, my dear," he said gently.

"So soon?" she asked. "Must I go now?"

Several others added their voices: "Please let Elsie stay, Mr. Dinsmore. Just another hour."

Horace was kind but firm. "Not tonight, for Elsie must follow the rules, but I have decided that she shall be allowed an extra hour tomorrow night." To Elsie he said, "I will be up in a while to tuck you in and get my good-night kiss."

Although the next day was Christmas Eve, Elsie followed her morning routine: first, her Bible reading and prayers; then, an early walk with her father, followed by breakfast, an hour at the piano, where she practiced a duet with Mary Leslie, and an hour of study in Horace's room. Mary Leslie, who seemed to believe that lessons were invented solely to torture children, was amazed at Elsie's eagerness for anything that resembled schoolwork.

Breakfast in the playroom had been a little difficult; several of the children were over-tired, and the little ones were especially peevish. Mrs. Brown, who had raised three children of her own before coming to Roselands, managed to keep the peace (though she secretly hoped the parents would see that their children had naps before the next meal).

Just when Elsie had finished her lesson with Horace, she was told that the Carrington family had arrived, and she rushed to the drawing room. Mrs. Carrington gave Elsie a warm embrace, remarking on how much she had grown since the previous summer. And Lucy and Herbert, the Carrington twins, both hugged their dear friend and expressed their joy at being all together again. Herbert suffered from a serious hip problem that made it hard for him to walk and often sapped his strength, but he assured Elsie that he was very much better these days. Still, he was tired after the long carriage ride, and his mother thought it best for him to rest, so she sent Elsie and Lucy off to find their other friends.

All the girls had a grand reunion in the playroom, and Elsie was happy to see Harry Carrington, one of Lucy's older brothers, there too. The younger children, however, were not being cooperative. Little Flora Arnott was soon in tears, for Enna — so spoiled that it never occurred to her to be polite to a guest — had taken most of the building blocks that Flora was playing with.

Elsie tried to solve the dispute, but Enna flatly refused to share — and Elsie knew better than to start a quarrel with Enna, who was Mrs. Dinsmore's pampered pet. Then Elsie had an idea. She took Flora aside and said, "Pay no attention to Enna. I have something that you will really enjoy playing with. Will you wait right here while I get it?"

Sniffling a little, Flora nodded her head. Elsie ran from the playroom and was back in just a few moments. Cradled in her arm, she carried a beautiful baby doll dressed in delicate white lace and linen. Gently, she put the porcelain baby in Flora's arms and said, "This is my very best doll, Flora, and you must be very careful with it. My guardian gave it to me when I was even younger than you. He's dead now, so this doll means a great deal to me."

27

Elsie's Impossible Choice

The little girl's blue eyes had widened with wonder. "Oh, Elsie," she said in almost a whisper, "I shall take very good care of it, I promise. It is so very pretty."

With that problem solved, Elsie rejoined her friends. They all went to her room to play and talk, and Elsie forgot all about the doll. When the dinner bell rang, she and Carrie and Lucy and Mary Leslie skipped back to the playroom. The first person they saw there was Flora, tears were streaming down her face. "Oh, Elsie," she cried, "I am so sorry about the doll! Enna tried to grab it from me, and it fell and broke! And I can't fix it!"

The little girl pointed to the window seat where the doll lay, its head broken entirely off. Elsie could say nothing for the lump in her throat, but as she crossed the room to fetch her broken treasure, she caught a glimpse of Enna, sitting quietly in a corner, a book in her hands and a look of stubborn defiance on her face. But Elsie was too upset even to be angry; she retrieved the doll and could do no more than stare miserably at the pieces.

Mrs. Brown, who was managing the preparation of the luncheon table, saw what had happened. Coming to Elsie's side, she put her arm around the girl's trembling shoulders and said in a soft but cheerful voice, "Do you know, Elsie, that I believe we can fix your lovely doll? The head has broken off cleanly — see — and I have some excellent glue that should repair it almost as good as new."

Elsie looked up. "Do you really think so, Mrs. Brown?"

"I shall do my best," the kind lady replied with a reassuring smile. "As soon as we have all had lunch, I'll take it to my room and see what I can do. But you must come and eat now." She led Elsie to her seat at the table and filled her plate with fresh fruit and cakes. Seeing the little girl's doubtful look, Mrs. Brown explained, "These cakes are not at all rich, my dear, and they entirely meet your father's approval."

"Won't your father let you eat *anything* good?" asked Mary Leslie. "Is he cross with you?"

Before Elsie could answer, Lucy piped up, "Elsie's father is so hard on her. When I was here last summer, he never let her have anything sweet or tasty. He makes her drink milk instead of coffee and eat cold breads instead of hot, and she can't even have a bit of butter. I do think he is the *strictest* man I ever saw."

Elsie's face had turned a bright red as anger rose inside her. "That's not true, Lucy," she said with intense feeling. "My Papa only does what is best for me. And I can eat almost anything I want."

"He is quite correct, too," said Mrs. Brown. "Elsie's father takes excellent care of her, and I have noticed that she is much stronger and healthier since Mr. Dinsmore's return." Then the good housekeeper looked pointedly at Lucy Carrington. "You know that too much rich food and too many late hours can be very harmful to growing children."

Lucy blushed and looked down at her own plate, which she had piled high with muffins and creamy cakes.

"I think that Elsie's father loves her very dearly," said Carrie Howard soothingly. To Elsie, she added, "Anyone can see that just by the way he looks at you."

Carrie then proceeded to change the subject, and the girls were soon planning the rest of their day and laughing as usual. But Elsie did not wholly forget her angry feelings. Though some people said she was too meek for her own good, Elsie had a quick temper and often had to struggle to control it. She was truly grateful to Carrie and Mrs. Brown for their kind defense of her father.

The girls planned to take an afternoon walk, but first, they were asked to join the adults in the drawing room. Almost as soon as she walked in the door, Elsie was seized upon by a young woman she had never seen before. The woman, who was dressed in the latest fashion and very talkative, took Elsie to a sofa and kept her sitting there for what seemed a long time. She overwhelmed the child with hugs and flattery: "What lovely hair you have! What soft ringlets, and such a beautiful color! What a sweet girl you are! Such a fair complexion and those rosy cheeks! You are a perfect little beauty! And those eyes! Where did you get them, my dear? But I have only to look at your father to see where they came from!"

To Horace, who had just come toward them, the lady gushed, "Why, Mr. Dinsmore, you should be very proud of this lovely child. She is the very image of you."

Bowing slightly, Horace replied, "You are kind to flatter me, Miss Stevens, but flattery is rarely good for either children or grown-ups. I cannot see that Elsie bears the slightest resemblance to me or my family, although," he looked softly into his child's eyes, "she is very like her mother, and I wouldn't have it otherwise. But I am forgetting my errand. We're getting together a group to take a ride and would like you to join us, Miss Stevens."

"Oh dear," the young woman said anxiously, "have I time to dress?"

"The ladies are getting ready now," Horace responded, "and the horses will be at the door in a few minutes."

"Then I must hurry," said Miss Stevens, excusing herself and sailing out of the room.

Horace took the lady's place on the sofa, and hugging Elsie close, he said in a tone that could not be overheard, "It's sometimes wise, Daughter, not to believe that people mean everything they say. Some people talk in a thoughtless way, and while they may not intend to be untruthful, they say a great deal that they do not really mean. Praise for worthy deeds can be good, but believing silly flattery can only make a child conceited and vain."

In her innocence, Elsie said, "I don't pay much attention when people say such things, Papa. I know what the Bible says in Proverbs, that 'charm is deceptive, and beauty is fleeting.' And it tells us that 'whoever flatters his neighbor is spreading a net for his feet.' So I should try to stay away from that lady, shouldn't I, Papa?"

"Yes, dear, whenever you can do so without being rude," he said. "Now I must see to our guests and their horses." Horace ruffled her curls and rose to go. He did not, however, tell Elsie the thought that ran through his mind: "My child finds wisdom in the Bible, and I am again amazed at how often that book seems to protect her from evil influences." Somewhere deep within him was another thought: that he, too, might someday be in need of such a safeguard.

The youngest children caught it first. Then it spread to the older children, the servants, the guests, and finally even the elder Mr. Dinsmore. The spirit of Christmas Eve affected everyone.

Elsie's Impossible Choice

All day long, the heavy doors into the parlor had been tightly shut. Only a few people were allowed entrance — Mrs. Dinsmore, Adelaide, Pompey, and two others of the house servants. Time and again, they were seen going into the room, carrying mysterious boxes and bundles. Elsie, Carrie, and the older children knew what was happening, of course, but they all — even Arthur Dinsmore, who was usually the first to spoil a surprise — kept their silence around the little ones.

When supper in the playroom was over that evening, the children began to wander downstairs to the drawing room where their parents and the other guests were gathered. The drawing room was brightly lit with an abundance of candles, but brighter still was the sense of anticipation that hummed throughout the room. As the clock approached eight, everyone began to assemble — as if by some common order — in the entry hall outside the parlor. All conversation died down to no more than a soft whisper, and all eyes were soon directed to the portal behind which something exciting lay.

Suddenly, the parlor doors opened, seemingly of their own accord. The long room beyond was dim and apparently empty, save for a dazzling light at its far end, and the watchers gasped in astonishment. A thick pine tree, as tall as the room itself, was covered with hundreds of lighted tapers that glowed and twinkled like the night stars. As the servants rushed to light the sconces around the parlor walls, it became apparent that the tree was hung with countless small toys and colorfully wrapped presents tied to the pine branches with red and gold ribbons. Larger packages were arranged under the tree's lowest boughs.

When this brilliant sight had sunk in a bit, old Mr. Dinsmore signaled for everyone to enter the room. Chairs

32

were pulled forward for the older adults, and Mr. Dinsmore took his place before the tree. After several kind words of thanks to his wife for her beautiful decoration and skillful secret-keeping, he asked Adelaide to assist in the distribution of the gifts. Names were called, and there were presents for everyone. The children were soon busy with their new dolls and toy soldiers and picture books and games. Mary Leslie and Flora Arnott were fascinated with their beautiful wax dolls whose eyes could open and close. Carrie received a lovely gold chain from her mother and a pretty pin in the shape of a butterfly from Elsie. Lucy was especially thrilled with a silver bracelet, decorated in mother-of-pearl, from her parents. Elsie also received a bracelet from her Aunt Adelaide and a needle-case from Lora. Herbert Carrington shyly thanked Elsie for her gift, a leather-bound copy of Sir Walter Scott's *Ivanhoe*, an adventure that was a favorite of his. Everyone was happy with their presents, save Enna; she had taken to a corner to pout when she saw that Mary Leslie's new doll was larger than her own.

Names continued to be called, and Elsie heard her own once more. Adelaide, wearing a bright smile, came to her and slipped a beautiful diamond ring on her niece's finger. "It's from your father," Adelaide said and pointed discretely. "He is standing right over there."

Elsie went straight to Horace, who was standing a little apart from the merry scene. She held out her hand for him to see. "Oh, thank you so much, Papa. See how beautiful it is."

"Do you really like it, my dear?" he asked.

"It is the most beautiful ring I have ever seen."

"But perhaps there is something you would have liked better. You must tell me the truth."

Elsie's Impossible Choice

Elsie blushed and lowered her head. But she soon looked up again and seeing only love in her father's eyes, she summoned the courage to say, "There is only one thing I could have wanted more, and that is your portrait, Papa."

Far from being angry, Horace smiled broadly and swung his little girl off the floor and into his arms. "Well, darling," he laughed, "if you want a picture of me, then someday you shall have it."

At that moment his own name was called, and Adelaide came toward him with a slim, shiny object in her hand. It was a gold pen, its label carefully written in Elsie's hand.

"Do you like it, Papa?" Elsie asked.

"I do, very much, and I shall think of you every time I use it. But I thought you said you had no present for me."

Elsie laughed now. "I only said there was none for you among *my* bundles. Aunt Adelaide was keeping this for me."

And so the evening sped by. Refreshments were served, and Louise and Lora led the older children in a lively game of charades, in which some of the adults participated. Elsie was completely surprised when her father came to tell her that it was time for bed.

"Is it nine thirty already?" she asked in astonishment.

"It is just past ten o'clock," Horace replied, "and high time you were asleep."

Elsie had no complaints this night, for though she had enjoyed every minute of the party, she still had one task to attend to, and she needed her rest to complete it.

Despite her late night, Elsie woke the next morning when her clock chimed five. It was still dark and very cold, but she slipped out of bed, found her slippers and robe, and as

34

quietly as a mouse, retrieved a little package from her bed-side table. Tiptoeing so as not to disturb Aunt Chloe, who shared her young charge's room, Elsie slowly and carefully opened her door and left her room. Luckily, the pale, pre-dawn glow through the hallway window was just enough to guide her to her goal. Her father's door at the far end of the hall was unlocked, and she silently stole inside. The heavy carpet hid any sound of her footsteps as she approached his bed and laid her tiny package on the table where he was sure to see it when he first awoke. Returning with the same caution to her room, she hopped into bed, shivering until the thick covers warmed her. It was not many more minutes until she heard Aunt Chloe stirring. To the comforting sounds of her nursemaid dressing for the day and starting a warming flame in the fireplace, Elsie drifted back to sleep.

Soon after the full light of morning had dawned, Elsie felt herself being shaken gently.

"Time to rise, child, if you want to meet your father before you go to breakfast," Chloe was saying.

Elsie was quickly dressed, and Chloe had brushed and curled her hair, tying it with a red satin ribbon for Christmas. Elsie was sitting in her little rocker, reading her Bible verses. She had chosen the beautiful story of the birth of Jesus as told in the Book of Matthew. On this day when Christians everywhere were celebrating the birth of the Savior, the little girl marveled at God's great gift — that He loved the people He created so much that He sent His only Son to live on earth as a human being and to die for the sins of all mankind.

She had just finished her reading when she suddenly became aware of a shining object being lowered before her eyes.

Elsie's Impossible Choice

"You recognize that gentleman?" Chloe asked from her position behind Elsie.

The little girl's hand closed gingerly around the miniature painting. "It's my Papa!" she cried. "Oh, how good of him! Look, Aunt Chloe. It is just like him. Isn't he handsome?"

Chloe fastened the fine, gold chain that held the miniature around Elsie's neck. It was, in fact, the second chain Elsie wore. The little girl lifted the other, older miniature from her dress and held it side-by-side with the new. Her own beautiful mother, who had died so young, and her beloved father — now Elsie wore both her parents close to her heart.

She was not the only one to receive an unexpected gift that morning. When she entered her father's room a few minutes later, he immediately scooped her up and gave her a kiss, saying, "Well, my little Elsie, you presented me with quite a beautiful surprise. It's a wonderful portrait of you, and I am delighted with it. I shall carry it with me always."

"Will you, Papa?" Elsie asked, but in her excitement did not give him time to answer. "And I shall carry your image with me, too, right next to Mamma's. Oh, Papa, your miniature is just what I wanted!"

"You see, Daughter, I told you that you should have it someday, and today is that day," he laughed. "And as you know, I always keep my word."

CHAPTER

3

The Voices of Temptation

"No temptation has seized you except what is common to man. And God is faithful; He will not let you be tempted beyond what you can bear. But when you are tempted, He will also provide a way out so that you can stand up under it."

1 CORINTHIANS 10:13

*M*any of the guests had chosen to sleep late on Christmas morning, so Roselands was subdued after the previous evening's excitement. Horace had gone before breakfast to attend to some business on the plantation, and Elsie was heading to the playroom to see if any of her little friends were up when she passed an open door off the hallway. From it came the distinctive, and not altogether welcome, voice of Miss Stevens.

"Elsie, you lovely little creature. Come in and see what I have for you."

Reluctantly, Elsie entered the room, and Miss Stevens, chattering gaily, first insisted that Elsie take a seat and then began rummaging in a drawer. What she found there was a large package which, with the prettiest of smiles, she placed in Elsie's hands.

Such temptation! Elsie could see that the package contained all her favorite candies and treats, and she would dearly have loved to taste each and every one of them. But her Papa was very strict about what she ate and had instructed her never to take candy of any kind unless he gave his express permission.

Though she wanted to accept the gift, Elsie had to say, politely, "Thank you very much, Miss Stevens, but Papa has told me not to take candy from anyone. He does not approve of children eating sweets."

Miss Stevens pouted. "That's too bad," she said, "but surely you can have one or two pieces, at least. They are really delicious, and they can't possibly hurt you. Your father need never know."

Elsie's Impossible Choice

Elsie was surprised by this offer. "But Miss Stevens," she said, "God would know, and I would know. How could I look at my Papa if I deceived him?"

The lady laughed. "My dear child, I believe you are making a mountain from a molehill. I have deceived my father many times over such trifles, with no harm done. But I won't press you. In fact, I have something that I am sure you will want," she reached back into the same drawer from which the candy had come, "and I bought it particularly for you."

Taking the bag of candy from Elsie's hands, Miss Stevens replaced it with a beautifully bound book. Elsie's eyes grew round with delight, for books were her greatest pleasure. Still, she felt somewhat uncomfortable receiving a gift from someone she did not respect, and she made an effort to decline. Miss Stevens would hear none of it, and finally Elsie took the book with genuine gratitude. She began to turn the pages and could see that it was a very interesting book.

"Aren't the pictures beautiful, dear?" Miss Stevens asked. "And the stories are very good, too."

"I hope that I can read them," Elsie replied, "but Papa doesn't allow me to read anything until he has approved of it. I will have to wait until he returns to ask his permission."

"How strict your father is!" Miss Stevens remarked, wondering to herself if Horace would try to dominate a wife as he did his daughter.

"Never mind, child," Miss Stevens went on. "Come sit by me, and *I* will read one of the stories to you. That would be alright because *you* would not be reading."

"Thank you, Miss Stevens. I know you're being kind, but that would be disobeying all the same," Elsie said. She was becoming anxious that the lady would tempt her further, so closing the book and tucking it under her arm, she made her excuses — thanking Miss Stevens once more — and left to find her friends.

The other girls were gathered in the playroom, and they all agreed the book was quite beautiful. They spent some time pouring over the lovely engravings, but Elsie resolutely refused to read even a word without her father's approval.

She had her opportunity to ask later that morning when she found Horace in the drawing room, talking with Miss Stevens. Elsie didn't interrupt but waited at the far side of the room until her father noticed her. Leaving the lady on the sofa, Horace came across to his daughter. "What have you there?" he asked pleasantly.

Elsie handed the book to him, explaining, "It's a Christmas gift from Miss Stevens. May I read it, Papa?"

Horace didn't answer at first, but slowly turned the book's pages, taking sufficient time to study the text and form an accurate opinion of the content. At last he shut the book.

"I'm afraid you must be content with the pictures," he said gently, "for the stories are not appropriate for a girl your age. In fact, this book would not make good reading for anyone. Still, the illustrations are quite nice, and you may enjoy them all you like.

"I am so pleased that I can trust you to obey me," he added with a loving smile.

Elsie was naturally a little disappointed, but she had plenty of books to interest her, and she trusted her father's judgment. Giving him a bright smile in return, she took the book from his hand and left to rejoin her friends.

Miss Stevens had been watching this little scene very closely, straining to overhear Horace's words. As the door closed behind Elsie, Miss Stevens was biting her pretty lip with frustration and struggling to keep her composure. Her maneuver had failed. In truth, she had come to Roselands with the intention of winning Horace Dinsmore's heart; flattering and petting his little daughter were part of her plan of attack. But his disapproval of her gift was not promising. Still, Miss Stevens had great confidence in her charms and accomplishments. If she had lost this little battle, she was more determined than ever to win the war.

In the hallway, Elsie found someone who immediately put thoughts of Miss Stevens and the book out of her mind. Her father's closest friend — now one of her own friends, too — had just arrived. On seeing Edward Travilla, Elsie ran to give him a welcoming kiss.

"Thank you, Miss Elsie," he said with a hearty laugh. "I assume that kiss was my Christmas present, so I owe you a gift in return."

He drew a small box from his pocket, which he opened to reveal a small gold thimble. "I know your Aunt Adelaide is teaching you to embroider," he said, "and my mother said this would be a suitable encouragement. It is also from her."

"Oh, thank you, Mr. Travilla, and please thank your mother as well. I must show it to Papa."

She ran back into the drawing room, Edward following, and went straight to Horace to display her gift. With a nod at Edward that included Miss Stevens as well, Horace remarked on how kind all his friends were to his daughter.

"So," Miss Stevens thought to herself with smug satisfaction, "he does like the attention I paid to his child after all."

But Elsie's attention was directed to Edward Travilla, for that gentleman was just inviting her and her friends to take a carriage ride with him after dinner. Promising to be waiting on the portico steps at precisely two o'clock, Elsie ran away to tell the other girls about their invitation.

Carrie, Lucy, and Mary Leslie fairly bubbled with anticipation, for Mr. Travilla was a great favorite with all the children. Finishing their dinner as quickly as possible, the girls scattered to get dressed for their ride, but Elsie could not find Aunt Chloe in her room or anywhere else in the house. In fact, Chloe had gone to the servants' quarters to deliver some gifts to the older servants, but Elsie, thinking her nursemaid might be in the kitchen, ran down the back steps and out to that building. The servants were very busy cleaning the stacks of dishes and utensils from dinner — a full house meant heavy labor for the staff — and no one noticed Elsie enter. Over the clattering of plates and the banging of pots, Elsie could hear that a lively conversation was underway.

The first words Elsie caught were from Aunt Phoebe, the plantation's excellent cook: "You don't know what you're saying, Pompey. Mr. Horace marry that bit of fluff and finery? No such thing! He's got more sense."

Then Pompey replied, "If Mr. Horace doesn't like her, then why have they been out riding every day? Haven't I seen him sitting with her morning, noon, and night, laughing and talking all the time? Haven't I seen her kissing Miss Elsie and calling her 'pretty creature' and 'sweet child' and the like?"

Elsie's Impossible Choice

The cook snorted disdainfully. "That woman may be playing up to Miss Elsie. But I tell you, Pomp, Mr. Horace has more good sense than to be taken in by her likes."

Another voice piped up, "Aunt Chloe doesn't believe a bit of it. She says Mr. Horace would never let a woman like that Miss Stevens take the place of his beautiful, dead wife."

But Pompey wasn't convinced. "Now, Aunt Chloe's a fine woman," he said, "but I don't suppose Mr. Horace is going to confide his matrimonial intentions to her. He's a young and handsome man, and it's about time he takes another wife."

Aunt Phoebe conceded that Miss Stevens was setting her cap for the younger Mr. Dinsmore, but she was sure he was too smart to be caught. Other voices added their opinions, but Elsie had heard enough, and though she didn't understand all of what was said, she returned to the house with a terrible feeling that something was about to take away the happiness that was still so new to her.

When she entered her room, Aunt Chloe was there.

"You must hurry, child," the nursemaid said. "The other girls and Mr. Travilla are waiting for you."

Chloe bustled about, getting Elsie into her coat and warm hat and scarf, and she took no notice of the little girl's quiet mood. On the carriage ride, Elsie tried to be her usual self; she laughed when Mary Leslie made her jokes and smiled at Lucy's endless chatter. Only Mr. Travilla sensed that something was bothering his young friend, but he decided that it was most likely the letdown that inevitably comes after several days of excitement and activity. Still, he determined to keep an eye on Elsie, in case her quietness might be the first sign of some illness.

That evening, the children joined the adults in the drawing room after supper. Elsie was hoping to have a few minutes alone with her father, but when she entered the room she saw that Horace was occupied. Miss Stevens was at the piano playing a difficult piece, and Horace leaned over her, turning the pages of the music and clearly enjoying her performance, for Miss Stevens was a gifted pianist.

Before Elsie's visit to the kitchen, this little scene would not have troubled her in the least, but now, it made her sick at heart. So anxious was she to catch her father's attention that she could hardly concentrate when Mrs. Carrington asked her about her Christmas presents and the afternoon's carriage ride.

Across the room, Edward Travilla was watching Elsie as she watched her father and Miss Stevens. It did not take many moments for him to guess the reason for Elsie's distracted mood. He knew that there was no reason for anxiety, that Horace had no interest in Miss Stevens except that of a good host. Naturally, Edward wanted to tell Elsie that her worries were for nothing, but he felt that this was a delicate subject and should be addressed by Horace himself. So he did the next best thing — he engaged Elsie and her three little friends in conversation and was soon entertaining them with his fascinating stories and several word games. Elsie seemed happy enough and joined in the fun, but every now and then her eyes wandered away to search out her father and Miss Stevens, and Edward caught the look of sadness and anxiety that passed across her face.

At length, Edward was summoned by some of the older ladies. The other girls went to their parents, and Elsie took this opportunity to slip quietly away from the lively gathering. Although her father had given her permission to stay up an extra half hour, she was suddenly very tired, and as she climbed the long staircase to her room, her arms and legs felt heavy indeed. A few tears trickled from her eyes, and she wiped them away quickly so that Aunt Chloe would not see.

When she was in her nightclothes, Elsie knelt to say her prayers, but it was not easy to gather her thoughts. In her heart, she had come to feel a real dislike for Miss Stevens, and she prayed earnestly for help to put these feelings away. Yet she also prayed that God would spare her and her father from the trial she feared: apart from her own feelings, she knew that Miss Stevens was neither truthful nor sincere, and Elsie feared for her father's happiness even more than her own.

As always, communing with her Heavenly Friend brought her comfort, and she felt better when Chloe helped her into bed. "Perhaps Papa will come and kiss me good-night," she murmured to herself as she lay her head on the pillow.

Down in the drawing room, however, Horace was engaged in an interesting conversation with several of the guests, and it was not until the clock struck ten that he missed his daughter. He consulted Lucy Carrington.

"Oh, Elsie left ages ago," Lucy informed him. "About eight thirty, I think. She looked tired, so she probably went to bed."

"Strange," Horace thought to himself, "that she did not bid me good-night." A little concerned now, he left the drawing room, and was followed by Edward Travilla.

"My friend," Edward said, halting Horace in the hall. "I think that your daughter is having some trouble tonight."

"What is it, Travilla?" Horace asked anxiously. "Is she sick? Has there been an accident?"

"No, no, Horace, nothing ails her physically. But servants will talk, you know, and children have eyes and ears, too. I was watching Elsie closely tonight, and I am sure she has picked up some wrong ideas about you and a certain lady."

"Gossip!" Horace exclaimed in vexation. "But are you certain that is Elsie's trouble? I wouldn't have such notions put into her head for money!"

"I am as sure as I can be without asking her directly. But it has been some time since she has looked so sad, and she could hardly take her eyes away from you and Miss Stevens tonight."

Horace shook his friend's hand warmly and thanked him before rushing upstairs.

Elsie was sleeping soundly when he entered her room, and Horace decided not to wake her, though he longed to assure her that all her fears were unfounded. "You will always be dearer to me than all the world," he whispered as he kissed her soft cheek.

Horace had a restless night, and he rose and dressed early to await his daughter. When her knock at his door came at exactly seven thirty, instead of bidding her to enter, as was his custom, he opened the door and took her into his arms.

"Elsie, darling," he said, looking closely into her face. "I missed you last night. You disappeared from the drawing room, and then you were asleep when I came to kiss you good-night."

"You did come, Papa?" Elsie said in genuine surprise. "I thought you were too busy."

"I'm never too busy for you, Daughter," he replied. Setting her on the floor, he kept her little hand in his and led her to his chair. Taking his seat, he lifted her to his knee and said, "Before we take our walk, I must talk to you. I believe that you were troubled last night, and I would like you to tell me why."

Elsie ducked her head, and softly she responded, "I'm afraid you'll be angry with me, Papa."

Gently, Horace assured, "I can never be angry with you when you speak from your heart, Elsie. But you must tell me honestly what concerns you, for I believe it concerns the both of us."

Elsie struggled to speak, but the words seemed to catch in her throat. Sensing her dilemma, Horace went on, "Elsie, you are more precious to me than anything in the whole, wide world. No one will ever take your place in my heart, and I would never marry anyone with whom you were not completely happy. I'm afraid that you have been disturbed by gossip, and I want you to believe that, whatever you heard, I have no intention of marrying Miss Stevens or any-one else."

Elsie listened to him with some amazement. "Can you read my thoughts, Papa?"

Horace laughed. "No, dear, but I can often read your face, and I can put two and two together and sometimes make a very good guess."

Her face, indeed, had brightened considerably at his words. Then she grew serious again. "Is it very naughty of me to think Miss Stevens a disagreeable woman? I felt she was from the first day she came here, Papa. I have tried to like her, but I just can't."

Horace struggled to put on a grave face as he said, "Well, darling, I am not the right person to reprove you for that. The truth is that I have much the same feeling about Miss

Stevens. But because we feel this way, we should go the extra mile to be kind to her, don't you think?"

Elsie considered for several moments, then agreed. Now that she knew her father was in no danger from the lady, Elsie discovered that she had some sympathy for Miss Stevens. After all, Elsie understood better than most what it felt like to be lonely.

Horace interrupted her thoughts with a jovial, "Well, no more about Miss Stevens! I have something for you that should make up for the storybook I denied you yesterday." He pointed to a pile of books on his writing table. Elsie jumped from his lap and ran across the room. The books were a series of historical biographies by Jacob Abbot, a writer whom Elsie enjoyed very much.

"Oh, Papa, these are so wonderful. I would like to read them all right now!"

Horace laughed. "I am glad they please, for it pleases me to have a child who enjoys reading so much. But we have a walk to take before you begin your new books. Run and get your coat and hat. I invited Mr. Travilla to join us this morning, and he is probably waiting outside for us and turning blue with cold."

Edward Travilla, who had the good sense to await his friends inside by the library fire, was delighted to see both Elsie and her father looking so carefree when they joined him. Each man took one of Elsie's mittened hands, and the three began their walk in a happy mood.

"I have an idea, Edward," Horace said as they reached the end of the long driveway. "I plan to take Elsie and the other girls on a horseback ride today. Perhaps you'd like to join us."

"That I would," Edward replied jovially, "if the young ladies have no objection. What do you say, Elsie? Do you

Elsie's Impossible Choice

young ladies like me enough to let me come along on your ride?"

"Oh, yes, Mr. Travilla," Elsie said with spirit. "You know that I like you next best to Papa, and I think the others like you even better."

"Take care," Edward said with mock sternness, "or you will hurt your father's feelings."

"No danger of that, my friend," Horace laughed, "so long as Elsie puts me first."

Carrie Howard was waiting in Elsie's room. "I'm so glad you're back," she exclaimed when Elsie entered. "Pompey has just brought the bracelet from town, and I wanted you to see how beautiful it is."

Indeed, the bracelet braided from Elsie's shiny curl was lovely. The braid work was extremely fine, and the maker had neatly attached delicate gold clasps.

"I'm sure Mamma will love it," Carrie said. "Since it was not ready for Christmas, I've decided to save it for a New Year's gift."

"That's a grand idea," Elsie agreed as she examined the bracelet carefully. "It really is lovely."

"Oh, by the way," Carrie said, "did you know that we are invited to a party tonight? The Carltons are giving it, and it's only for children. I think it will be so much fun to attend a party that's just for us. Don't you think so, Elsie?"

"It should be," Elsie replied, but had Carrie been paying closer attention, she might have heard a note of uncertainty in her friend's voice.

Later, when Elsie entered her father's room for her morning lesson, she had almost forgotten about the party, but before she could sit down, her father placed a white envelope in her hand.

"It's an invitation for you," Horace said, "to a party at the Carltons this evening. Would you like to go?"

Elsie turned the envelope over and over, considering her response. "Do you want me to go, Papa?" she asked at last.

"Only if that is what you like," he answered kindly. "Normally, I prefer to accompany you on any journey, even a short one, but this is an exception. All your friends will be going, but you must please yourself, my dear."

Elsie thought for a few moments more. "Then I'd like to stay at home, Papa, if you will be here," she said.

Horace couldn't help being pleased — he had genuinely come to enjoy his child's company at all times — but he wanted to be certain that his feelings didn't influence Elsie's decision. "It will be very quiet here tonight," he said. "I have some important letters to write, so I won't be able to give you my full attention."

"That's alright, Papa," Elsie responded happily. "I can read one of my new books, and I'll be very quiet." She looked into his face and added seriously, "It will be so nice to have one of our quiet evenings again."

Just after their mid-day meal, Elsie and her friends gathered in the drawing room. They had about an hour before their ride with Horace and Edward Travilla, and Adelaide had promised to teach the girls some new embroidery stitches. She was helping Carrie master the intricate skill of making French knots when Lucy Carrington pulled Elsie aside.

"Carrie showed me the bracelet she had made for her mother," Lucy said excitedly, "and it's just perfectly beautiful! But she wouldn't tell whose curls it was woven from. I'm sure I could never guess," she added with a wink. "Oh, Elsie, I so want to have a bracelet like that for my Mamma, and your hair would be just right for it. Won't you let me have just one of your curls? You have so many that one would never be missed!"

"I'm sorry, Lucy," came the deep voice of Horace Dinsmore, who had entered the room just in time to overhear Lucy's pleading. "You can't have one of my curls because I can't spare even one."

Lucy giggled. "Not one of *your* curls, Mr. Dinsmore. They're much too short for a bracelet."

"But, Miss Lucy, I heard you ask for one," Horace replied teasingly. "Perhaps you didn't know that my hair grows on two heads."

"But it was Elsie's curl I asked for," Lucy said in puzzlement.

"Elsie doesn't have any," Horace responded, "for they all belong to me. I let her wear them, of course, but she cannot give them away."

Lucy laughed at Horace's joke, then turned her attention back to her sewing. But Elsie was so troubled that her hand shook as she tried to make her stitches. "I must tell Papa that I did give away one of my curls," she was thinking to herself. "I should have known he would care. Last summer, he wouldn't let me get my hair cut. Why didn't I remember that? Oh, what if he is very angry with me?"

Then, as if another voice were speaking to her, she heard the words, "Don't tell him, then. He will never know."

"I must tell him," Elsie thought with resolve.

But the voice continued, "Then tell him tomorrow. If you tell him now, he will punish you by making you stay home from the ride."

Back and forth, Elsie struggled with the voice of Temptation. As the battle raged within her, she hardly noticed when Mary Leslie exclaimed, "It's almost time for our ride! We must get dressed."

Abstractedly, Elsie said, "I have to speak to Papa first. You go on, and I'll come in a few minutes."

As the other girls bounded merrily from the room, Elsie slowly approached her father, who had seated himself on the sofa to read his newspaper. Becoming aware of her approach, he asked, "What is it, Daughter?"

In spite of her best efforts, tears gathered in her eyes and a bright flush rose to her cheeks. "Oh, Papa," she said in a hesitating voice. "Please don't be angry with me. I didn't know that you cared so much for my curls, and I gave one to Carrie for her mother's bracelet. I didn't think about them belonging to you."

Horace was very much surprised by this outburst, but his tone was gentle. "No, dearest, I won't be angry this time. I understand that you didn't know how much I care about everything that affects you — even your pretty curls."

Elsie's relief was enormous. "I'll never do it again, Papa. I promise," she said with intensity. "But I know you must punish me. I was afraid to tell you at first because I thought you wouldn't let me go riding with you."

Horace searched her face. "Then why didn't you delay your confession until after our ride?" he questioned. Elsie had begun to tremble again, but her father's voice was kind and reassuring.

Elsie blushed. "I wanted to wait, Papa, but I knew that would be wrong."

Horace gathered her in his arms and said, "Dear Elsie, I am proud of you for your honesty and truthfulness. You have done what is right, and I'd never think of punishing you for that. Of course you shall have your ride, and when we return, you shall also have this."

He reached into his pocket and took out an envelope, which he handed to Elsie.

"It's from Miss Allison!" Elsie said with excitement. "Can I read it now?"

"It's time you got into your riding clothes," Horace laughed, "or you will be left behind. Save the letter till this evening. If you are to stay home with me, you will need something to read. Now hurry up to Aunt Chloe, and I will attend to the horses."

The afternoon's ride was every bit as much fun as the girls expected. Edward Travilla entertained them with his stories; Horace added several tales about his time in Europe; and near the end of the ride, Carrie whispered something to Elsie that pleased her greatly.

"Do you know that I like your father quite as much as Mr. Travilla?" Carrie began. "Your Papa is so kind to us, Elsie, and it's clear he loves you more than anything."

Elsie almost glowed with delight, though she said nothing.

The rest of the afternoon passed just as pleasantly, and after an early supper, Elsie helped all her friends dress in their prettiest gowns. They were naturally surprised at her not attending the party, and Lucy, whose opinion of Horace Dinsmore was not nearly so high as Carrie's, decided that he must be keeping Elsie at home for a punishment of some kind. But it was with relief that Elsie finally watched the two carriages full of the children depart from Roselands. The house was very quiet when she entered the library. Her father was seated at his desk, bent over his writing. She had brought one of her new books, and she drew a small stool next to the desk and sat down to read. For some time, the only sounds she heard were the soft scratching of her father's pen as it scurried across the paper and the crackling of the fire that warmed the room.

She was deeply involved in her book when her father addressed her. "Elsie dear," he was asking, "are you enjoying what you are reading?"

She looked up from the pages that had already caught her imagination. "Oh, yes, Papa, it is a very interesting story, and all the better for being real."

Horace smiled, then said, "Perhaps you can take a small break to read something else. Did you bring your letter from Miss Allison?"

"Yes, sir, I have it here," she replied, drawing the neat white envelope from her pocket. "May I read it to you, Papa?"

"Only if that's what you like, Daughter. It is your letter, and you need not share it with me."

"But I want to, Papa," Elsie protested. "Miss Allison was always so good to me, and she writes such nice letters."

In truth, Horace was curious about Miss Rose Allison. He knew that her father was an old friend of his father's, that the family lived in Philadelphia, and that Miss Allison had spent several months as a house guest at Roselands before Horace had returned home the previous spring. Adelaide had told him how the young lady had taken a sincere interest in Elsie and befriended the little girl. He knew as well that Miss Allison was a dedicated Christian. Horace himself paid little more than lip-service to the practices of established religion and tended to regard most Christians as shallow and irrational. But because he had already experienced the strength of his daughter's faith, he was not so inclined to pre-judge Rose Allison as he once might have been.

"Then I would like to hear your letter," he told Elsie, "and later, perhaps I can help you with your reply."

Elsie carefully unfolded the crisp, white pages and began to read. It was a cheerful letter, well suited to the interests of a child. Miss Allison gave a lively account of life at her home, of the activities of her little brothers and sisters, of the gifts that they planned to give one another for Christmas. At the close of the letter, Miss Allison referred to Elsie's earlier writings and expressed her own joy in her little friend's new happiness.

"I am so glad," the letter ran, "that your father now loves you so dearly. My heart ached for you when I read of your disappointment when you first met him. You never said you were disappointed, but I recognized a tone of sadness in your letters then. Because I knew how much you yearned for his return and his affection, I could not help but guess the reason. So now you can rejoice in your *earthly* father's love. And never forget your *Heavenly* Father, for He is the giver of all good gifts, including the precious love of your Papa. Keep close to Jesus, for His love is the only *truly* satisfying love, and remember that He will never fail you."

Elsie finished reading and waited for her father to say something, but he was quiet, seeming to be lost in thought. After many moments, Horace looked at his child, a soft smile on his lips, and said, "It is a very nice letter, Elsie. But Miss Allison seems to warn you not to trust too much in my affection. You must never be afraid of losing my love, child. Even if you should become very naughty and troublesome, you will always be a part of myself and your dear, lost mother."

A serious look came into Elsie's eyes at his words, and she said with great earnestness, "If ever I am very bad, I hope you will punish me as severely as you must, but please, Papa, promise that you will never stop *loving* me!"

Horace lifted her onto his lap and hugged her tenderly. "Put your mind at rest, dearest Elsie. I could never stop loving you, even if I wished. You are part of my heart, and that will never change."

Elsie lay her head on his shoulder, and for some time, father and daughter sat together in the quiet warmth of their love. As the fire burned lower, Elsie's eyelids grew heavy, and she drifted into a sweet, sound sleep. Horace raised her in his arms and gently carried her to her room, delivering her to the care of Aunt Chloe.

He went back to the library, intending to read, but his attention kept returning to his child. It troubled him that Elsie still needed the reassurance of his love and affection so often. If he had known how to pray, Horace might have asked that Elsie's trust in his love would always be as simple and pure as it was this evening. But he was satisfied that his own assurances would be enough for her. In his self-confidence, Horace never imagined that the hardest test of love could fall on him.

CHAPTER

4

A Near Disaster

"Jesus said, "Father, forgive them, for they do not know what they are doing."

LUKE 23:34

A Near Disaster

In the children's playroom, breakfast was late the next morning, and some of the young people were still tired after the excitement of the Carltons' party. Arthur Dinsmore was in a particularly bad mood. A dark shadow seemed to hang about him, and he spoke to no one except when Harry Carrington whispered something in his ear. Whatever Harry said, it drew an angry shout from Arthur, who jumped from the table and stormed out of the room.

A little later, Elsie was in her bedroom, gathering together her books for her morning lesson with her father. She didn't notice that her door had been opened and someone had entered until she felt a cold hand on her shoulder. She jumped and turned around. When she saw that it was Arthur, she was extremely annoyed. Of all her young aunts and uncles, Arthur had always been the most unkind to her, and Elsie tried to avoid his company whenever possible.

"What do you want?" she demanded. "Papa is waiting for me."

"He can wait a few minutes more," Arthur sneered. Then his face softened into something like a smile. "I need your help, little Elsie. I need some money, and I know you can lend it to me. I saw your purse the other day, and you had at least five dollars in it. That's exactly what I need — five dollars."

"What for?" she asked, holding in her irritation that he should have looked into her purse.

"That's none of your business," Arthur snapped. "I need it *now*, and I will pay you back next month. That's all you need to know."

"But I can't lend you money," Elsie said, as nicely as possible. "Papa has forbidden me to, and I can't disobey him."

Arthur knew full well how low he stood in his elder brother's opinion, and that made him angrier still. "You weren't so careful about obeying your father last summer. Remember when he asked you to play the piano on that Sunday and you wouldn't do it? You didn't care about following his orders then."

"That was different! It meant disobeying God's command on the Sabbath," Elsie retorted hotly.

Struggling with his own anger, Arthur got himself under control once more. In a pleading tone, he went on, "But I must have the money, and you're the only one who can help me. I have to pay a debt, Elsie. To Dick Percival. I owed him a dollar, and last night I tried to win it back, but I lost even more. Now I owe him five, and Dick says that if I don't pay him today, he will tell Papa or Horace and get the money from them. But I haven't a cent of my own, and you know that Mamma won't help me. It's useless to ask my sisters because they never have any money to spare. You have to give it to me, Elsie!"

As he spoke, Elsie had shrunk back from him. In shock, she raised her hand to her face and exclaimed, "Gambling! Oh, Arthur, how could you gamble? How could you do anything so wicked? You have to tell Grandpa and ask him to forgive you. He'll understand if you tell him the truth, Arthur."

"Never! I can never tell him!" Arthur shouted. His face had turned a deep red, and his eyes seemed to blaze with his fury. Before Elsie could react, he stepped forward and grabbed her wrist, twisting it painfully. "You have to give me the money now! You're my only hope!"

Elsie wanted to scream; instead she spoke as clearly and forcefully as she could. "Let me go this instant, Arthur. If you hurt me, Papa will find out, and he won't let you get away without punishment."

This reminder of his brother's power stopped Arthur. His face turned pale, and savagely he threw Elsie's arm aside.

"Besides," Elsie went on in as calm a voice as she could manage, "I have to record everything I spend in my expense book for Papa to check. He would see that I gave you money, and then he'd know about your debt."

"But you could easily cover it up," Arthur said. "You could add a bit here and there to your expenses, and Horace would never know the difference. I could do it for you," he added hopefully. "I could fix up your book to hide five dollars."

"But that would be lying, Arthur, and I never lie to Papa. You must tell the truth yourself."

At this, Arthur's anger rose again. His eyes narrowed to slits, and he seemed about to reach for Elsie again. But at the moment, footsteps echoed from the hallway, and Arthur turned to listen until the steps disappeared. Shooting one, last, fierce glance at his niece, Arthur left the room, slamming the door behind him. Alone, Elsie suddenly found herself trembling. Would Arthur really have hurt her? She didn't think so. But never before had she seen him so angry and desperate. She tried to turn her thoughts to something else and had at least calmed her shaking when Aunt Chloe entered a few minutes later.

"Your Papa sent me with a message," the nursemaid said, apparently noticing nothing awry with her young charge. "He can't study with you this morning because a gentleman has come to do some business. He says he's very sorry, but he'll take you for a long ride this afternoon."

Elsie's Impossible Choice

Normally, Elsie would have been disappointed to miss her private hour with her father, but now she felt only gratitude. His absence gave her time to think — and she had much to think about. Whether he realized it or not, Arthur had shared a terrible secret with her, and she had to decide whether to tell her father and grandfather. More than anything, she hated to tell tales on others. (She had been hurt more often than she cared to remember by the tattling of others, especially Enna and Arthur, who frequently, before Horace's return, used half-truths and falsehoods to cause trouble for her.) But gambling, she knew, could ruin Arthur's whole life. Was it her duty to inform on him? She thought back over everything he had said and remembered his remark that she was his only hope. If that were true — and she could imagine no one else who would help Arthur — then he would have no choice but to go to Mr. Dinsmore. Thinking how much better it would be if Arthur made his own confession, she finally decided to keep his secret to herself.

The next week passed without any serious incident. Elsie enjoyed the company of her friends, for she and the other girls always had fun together. Horace treated them to pony rides, and there were several trips into the city. Adelaide continued the embroidery lessons, and Mrs. Brown taught the girls and Herbert Carrington, who was still weak and confined to the house, some interesting new games.

There were the inevitable little trials, of course. The younger children seemed to grow more restless and irritable as the days went by, and Elsie was often called on to mediate their disputes, though there was little she could do about Enna's selfishness. Mrs. Dinsmore remained as cold to Elsie as ever, but the woman always hid her disdain when other adults were around. Elsie had learned to be alone with her step-grandmother as little as possible and to be especially polite when they were together. Sometimes she wondered why Mrs. Dinsmore was so hateful to her, but now that she had the security of her father's love, Mrs. Dinsmore's attitude no longer troubled her as it once had. Horace missed no more of the morning lessons with his daughter, and even though he was busy with the guests, he made a point to spend time with her each evening before her bedtime.

Of Arthur, Elsie saw very little except at mealtimes. He was more quiet than she could remember, and when she occasionally caught his eye, she could read his terrible anger there. Still, she hoped that he had spoken to her grandfather, for she felt the heavy weight of knowing his dreadful secret.

The last day of the old year dawned brightly, and as if to welcome in the new year with good cheer, the weather turned warm, and the sky cleared. The children decided to take a walk after dinner, and with one exception, it was a lively and laughing group that left Roselands that afternoon. Horace had instructed the older children where it was safe to go and which paths to follow. He also sent along Jim, the young servant who had long since demonstrated his dependability as a guardian, to keep a watchful eye on the group.

In winter, the plantation was a much different place. The only green came from the pine trees; the vast fields, where cotton and corn would grow, were bare and brown. But there was still much to see and do, and the girls helped the little children gather seed pods and pine cones, gum nuts and dried branches to build a fairy castle. When at last the light began to fade, they called everyone together for the walk home, counting heads to be sure that everyone — even Arthur — was accounted for.

With Jim at the rear to gather up any stragglers, they followed a path that took them over a steep hill, and Elsie and Carrie were the first to reach the top, with Arthur and Harry Carrington close behind them. The two girls had stopped to take in the spectacular view of the plantation and Roselands rising in the distance when Arthur came running up. In an instant, he managed to shove Elsie hard, and she slipped on a patch of dried moss and lost her balance. She felt her feet give way and, with a pitiful cry of fear, tumbled down the opposite side of the hill. Carrie could only watch in horror as her friend rolled helplessly down the rocky, scrubby slope. At the bottom, the little body finally stopped and lay perfectly, terribly still.

The other children, who had just crested the hill, saw where Elsie lay, and Carrie, Lucy, Harry, and Mary Leslie ran down the path to their friend. Carrie knelt; gently she untied Elsie's bonnet strings and used the soft hat as a pillow for Elsie's head. The little children had joined them, and several were crying, so Lucy and Mary Leslie took them aside. But they had all seen Elsie's face, so deathly white, and her closed eyes.

Carrie called out, "Hurry, Jim, and go for the doctor! Harry, you run for her father as fast as you can! Lucy, stop crying right this instant and tend to the children! Does anyone have smelling salts?"

Jim and Harry were on their way almost before the words left Carrie's mouth. Mary Leslie dug into her pocket and brought out a small, amber bottle that she had received as a Christmas present.

"Here!" she cried, handing the bottle to Carrie. "Oh, is she dead?"

"No, but she is hurt," Carrie replied as she uncorked the bottle and passed it quickly beneath Elsie's nose. As the sharp scent of ammonia escaped the bottle, Elsie's eyelids fluttered, and Carrie felt a tremor of relief. But it was short-lived: the little eyes closed again as Elsie fell back into unconsciousness.

"Shouldn't we try to lift her off the cold ground?" Mary Leslie asked.

"No!" Carrie replied firmly. "We mustn't move her till her father or the doctor arrives."

Although they were only a quarter mile or so from the house, it seemed an eternity before Horace, with Harry at his side, pulled up in the carriage. Jumping to the ground, he rushed to his child. In spite of his fear, Horace gently tried to ascertain the extent of Elsie's injuries. As he felt her little arms for signs of a break, Elsie again opened her eyes and smiled faintly at the sight of her father.

"Hello, Papa," she whispered.

"My darling girl," he said softly. "Are you in pain?"

"Yes, Papa," she answered feebly. "My ankle hurts, and my head, too."

Horace gently touched her ankle, and Elsie winced and moaned. But he could tell the ankle was not broken, and so Horace carefully gathered her into his arms and began to walk back to the carriage.

"How did this happen?" he asked Carrie, who was at his side.

"I didn't see, sir," the girl said. Then she looked at the huddle of frightened children. "Did any of you see how Elsie fell?"

Elsie's Impossible Choice

Horace added his own question: "Who was nearest to her?"

Several little voices said at once, "Arthur."

Horace searched the faces until, at the back of the group, he spotted his younger brother. Arthur was struggling to keep his countenance impassive, but Horace knew him too well. He could read fear in his brother's eyes, and something else. Angry defiance.

"Will you never be satisfied," Horace demanded, looking straight at Arthur, "until you have killed my child?"

A groan from Elsie brought Horace back. With great tenderness, he lifted her into the carriage and entered himself. Instructing the driver to proceed as carefully and quickly as he could, Horace cradled Elsie in his lap, supporting her injured ankle, for the ride home.

The doctor was already there, and when Elsie had been placed on the sofa in the library, he quickly examined his young patient. In a few minutes he was able to deliver good news to Horace: Elsie had only a badly sprained ankle and a slight bruise on her head. He reassured the worried father that there were no broken bones and no sign of any damage to her spine, and he began to wrap the ankle in strong gauze.

As Elsie lay on the sofa, she seemed almost her old self. The color had come back to her face, and although her leg hurt badly, she was smiling at her father.

"Tell me how you fell, dear," Horace urged.

"Must I, Papa? I'd rather not," she pleaded.

Horace was too grateful to have his daughter safe to push for an answer, so he let the matter drop. Besides, he was sure he already knew the cause of her injury.

When the ankle had been wrapped and instructions given for Elsie's care, the doctor remarked kindly on her patience and courage before he rose to leave. At the front door, how-ever, he paused to say one more thing to Horace alone. "That's a sweet child you have," he began. "I don't see how anyone could want to harm her. But believe me, Horace, there has been foul play somewhere. She did not fall with-out help. I would get to the bottom of it, if I were you."

"That I shall, Doctor Barton, I promise," Horace replied. "But are you sure her ankle is not seriously injured?"

"Trust me, my good man. I am confident there will be no permanent damage if she is made to stay off the ankle until it is completely healed. She must not walk on it for several weeks. I know you will see that she is carefully tended to. And don't worry too much. You needn't be overly anxious."

Horace smiled and grasped the good-hearted doctor's hand firmly before bidding him good-bye.

After checking that Elsie was comfortably in Aunt Chloe's care and ordering that supper for himself and his daughter be served in the library, Horace hurried to the drawing room where everyone — especially the children — awaited news. Horace informed them all that Elsie would be fine; he also explained that she would not be able to walk for some time. He was firm that everyone should be careful not to let Elsie stand or walk or further damage her leg. Horace also gave particular thanks to Carrie for her cool head in the crisis, and once everyone had expressed their understand-ing of the doctor's orders and their best wishes for Elsie, Horace went back to his daughter. But he had not failed to notice that one person was missing from the gathering in the drawing room.

Elsie's Impossible Choice

The children's walk back to Roselands had been difficult indeed. Before departing, Horace had put Carrie and Harry in charge, and they tried as best they could to quiet the others' fears. Soon they were all — all except Arthur, who walked well behind the rest — discussing what had happened.

"I'm sure Arthur pushed her," Lucy said. "He hates her like poison, and he's been angry with her about something for days now. I've seen it in his eyes every time he looks at her. It started, let's see, back on the day after the Carltons' party. Oh, and I remember hearing him shouting at her that morning. They were in Elsie's room, and I went up to get a book from her. But when I got to the door, I heard Arthur yelling, so I left."

"But what has that got to do with her falling?" Mary Leslie asked. "Arthur always seems to be angry at somebody."

"Don't be stupid," Lucy said thoughtlessly. "It shows that something was wrong between them. That means Arthur had a *motive*!" she declared as if the matter were settled.

"Well, I don't know why anyone would be so cruel to Elsie," Carrie said.

"Nor I," Harry agreed. "But the more I think of it, the more certain I am that Arthur must have pushed her. I remember just where she was standing, and there's no way she could have fallen like that on her own. She had to be pushed. And then look at how guilty Arthur acted when Elsie's father came. Still, it may have been an accident."

"Oh, I should be very frightened if Elsie's father looked at me the way he looked at Arthur," Mary Leslie said with a little shiver.

"Looks can't hurt," Harry observed wisely, "but I wouldn't want to be in Arthur's shoes. I imagine Mr. Dinsmore will do something a good deal worse than *look* before he is done with Arthur."

Lucy Carrington, who always wanted to be first with any news, whether it be good or bad, rushed to her mother's room as soon as the children got back to the house. Herbert, who had felt ill that day, was lying on the couch, and Mrs. Carrington sat nearby, reading to him. Breathlessly, Lucy blurted out the story of Elsie's fall, ending with the declaration that "Arthur did it, and I'm sure he did it on purpose, too. He's so mean and wicked that I expect he'll kill her someday!" Then she burst into tears. "He ought to be in jail!"

"What are you saying, my dear?" Mrs. Carrington asked in confusion and alarm. Equally startled by his sister's outburst, Herbert demanded, "Is she hurt? Is Elsie hurt?"

Through her sobs, Lucy managed to explain that Horace had brought Elsie home and that the doctor was with them. "Oh, Mamma, if you could have seen the look that Mr. Dinsmore gave Arthur!"

"But why would Arthur want to hurt a sweet and gentle girl like Elsie?" Mrs. Carrington asked as she wiped Lucy's tears with her handkerchief.

"I think I know," came a small voice from the couch. Mrs. Carrington turned to Herbert, who had gone very pale.

"Why didn't I say something before?" he went on with a shudder. "I might have saved Elsie."

"Whatever do you mean, Herbert?" his mother inquired anxiously.

Herbert straightened up, and his voice grew stronger. "I will tell you, Mamma; then you must tell me what to do. Remember that I didn't go to the Carltons' party but stayed home and rested? Well, the next day, I felt very well, so I went out for a walk with the others. Elsie wasn't with us, and I'm so slow that pretty soon everyone was ahead of me. I got tired, so I sat down by some bushes to rest. And that's when I heard Arthur talking to someone. I didn't mean to eavesdrop, but they were on the other side of the bushes. I even whistled to let them know I was there, but they didn't seem to care. And they were talking so loudly. The other person was a boy named Bob who's a friend of Dick Percival's. It turns out that Arthur owes Dick Percival a gambling debt — they called it a debt of *honor* — and this Bob was supposed to collect it.

"Well, Arthur acknowledged that he owed the money and had promised to pay that day. He said he tried to borrow it from someone else. He didn't say Elsie by name, but he did say *she* wouldn't lend him anything without telling *Horace*. Then he said *she* was just making excuses, that *she* never did him any favors, and someday he'd make *her* very sorry. I could hear that he was very angry.

"Then they talked some more, and the other boy finally agreed to give Arthur until New Year's Day to settle the debt. That's when Arthur gets his allowance."

At this, Herbert turned tear-filled eyes to his mother. "What should I do, Mamma? Is it my duty to tell Arthur's father?"

Mrs. Carrington, who felt almost as much affection for Elsie as her own children, replied firmly but lovingly, "Yes, son, because Mr. Dinsmore must know about Arthur's gambling so that he may put a stop to it. And if Arthur escapes punishment this time, he may put Elsie in danger again. I am sorry it must be you who overheard that conversation, but we must all do our duty, son, even when it is disagreeable and when our motives may be misunderstood."

Herbert sighed deeply. "Should I tell him now?" he asked.

Mrs. Carrington considered carefully. "No," she said at last. "I think Horace will investigate and perhaps he may find the truth without your assistance. If not, then tomorrow will be time enough."

At this brief reprieve, the color returned to Herbert's face and he settled back on the couch. He would not have Elsie hurt for the world, but unlike his sister, he never relished being the bearer of bad news.

It was not until supper that the senior Mr. Dinsmore, who had been away for the day, heard the news of Elsie's injury. The children had reported to their parents that Arthur was at fault, and several of the adults conveyed this information to their host.

Mr. Dinsmore was greatly angered, for he detested all forms of cowardice. Horace came into the dining room just as the meal was ended, and as the guests went to their different duties, Mr. Dinsmore took his eldest son into the library for a private conversation. When they were alone, old Mr. Dinsmore asked about Elsie's condition.

"She has been pretty badly hurt, Father," Horace said, "and is in a good deal of pain, though she will recover."

Mr. Dinsmore began to pace the room, as was his habit in times of stress. "Well, is it true that Arthur had a hand in this business?" he wanted to know.

Horace, keeping his voice even and calm, replied, "I have no doubt of it, sir. The children all agree that he was closest to her when she fell. Elsie has begged not to tell what happened, and Arthur remains silent, but neither of them has denied that he pushed her. The truth, Father, is that I have reason now to fear for my child. I have made up my mind that either Arthur must be sent away to boarding school or I must take Elsie and make a home for us elsewhere."

This declaration shocked Mr. Dinsmore, for he both loved and depended on his eldest son. "Surely this is too important a decision for you to make so suddenly," he declared.

"It is not so sudden, Father. For some time, I've suspected that Elsie has been forced to put up with a great deal of ill treatment from both Enna and Arthur, as well as my stepmother. Elsie never complained, so it was only gradually that I came to see how unjustly she has been treated by those whom I expected to show her at least common kindness.

"The incident this afternoon is just the last in a long line of abuses she has endured. And it is a mercy that she was not killed or crippled for life." At this, Horace's voice broke, and he dropped his face into his hands.

His father came to his side and put a warm arm around his shoulder. "We must not worry ourselves about what might have been," the older man said. "We must take precautions that it should never happen again. But you can't think of leaving Roselands, not unless you plan to marry again. And I don't think that is your plan."

"No indeed, sir," Horace said, "but I will protect my child. I am all that she has."

"I know that we haven't shown her all the kindness we ought," Mr. Dinsmore admitted, "but I was not aware of the abuses you describe. I shall certainly speak to my wife, and Arthur will be sent to school. It's something I've wanted to do for a long time. He's in constant trouble and is much too difficult for the governess to handle. But Mrs. Dinsmore has opposed it — you know how she dotes on the boy — and I've given in to her to keep the peace. Well, that is over. I'm so ashamed of him, attacking a small girl. You were always headstrong yourself, Horace, as a boy, but I never knew you to do a mean or cowardly thing."

Horace looked at his father kindly. He knew how much this affair disturbed the old gentleman, for Mr. Dinsmore was above all a man of honor.

"Thank you, Father," he said. "But to be fair to Arthur, I think we should conduct an open investigation. I know Elsie will not speak against him, but perhaps we can get the true story from the other children."

Mr. Dinsmore agreed and immediately summoned a servant, intending to call all the children to a meeting in the drawing room. But at Horace's suggestion, he sent first for Arthur, hoping that the boy might make his own confession. It was useless. Arthur denied everything, claiming that Elsie had merely slipped and that he had been nowhere near her. Believing that Elsie would say nothing and that no one else could prove him to be guilty, Arthur stubbornly stood his ground and continued his bluff — even when threatened with public humiliation in front of the guests.

"Then you leave me no choice," Mr. Dinsmore said sadly. He called for a servant, and this time instructed that the entire household be invited to assemble.

Twenty minutes later, all the children had joined their parents when Mr. Dinsmore, Horace, and Arthur entered the drawing room. The room was filled with a strange and somehow unpleasant air of expectation. The young people guessed that this gathering had some connection to Elsie's accident, and the little ones wiggled with nervous excitement. Carrie and Harry, however, sat silently, both with grave expressions on their faces. Lucy — who had not betrayed her own brother's secret to anyone — could not resist whispering behind her hand to Mary Leslie, while Herbert clung to his mother's hand. The chatting and giggling continued for a few seconds and then, at no one's command, suddenly died away. The room became almost as still as if it were empty.

Mr. Dinsmore at last broke the tense silence. In as normal a voice as he could muster, he asked, "Can any of you children tell me who was closest to Elsie when she fell this afternoon?"

Several young voices replied, "Arthur, sir."

"I see," Mr. Dinsmore said. "Was anyone else near her? Carrie Howard, I notice that you and Elsie are often together. Did you see what happened?"

Carrie spoke up clearly. "I was there, Mr. Dinsmore, quite near her. But I had turned away to look at something in the distance, so I didn't see her when she fell. But I'm certain she was not near enough to the edge to have fallen over by herself."

"Thank you for your honest reply, Carrie." Mr. Dinsmore looked to another of the young people. "Harry Carrington, someone has told me that you were with Arthur when Elsie was injured. I want you to be frank and tell me exactly what my son did."

Harry was flushing deeply and wishing he were anywhere at this moment but in this room. Still, he was a truthful young man, and what had happened to Elsie troubled him greatly. With only a little hesitation, he explained, "Yes, sir, I was near Arthur, and I think he must have pushed Elsie, but I believe it may only have been an accident."

"I wish that were so," Mr. Dinsmore said, almost under his breath. "Does anyone know if Elsie has angered Arthur in some way or if he has displayed unkind feelings toward her?"

Walter Dinsmore, who was normally the quietest of all the Dinsmore children, suddenly spoke up. "Yes, Papa," he declared. "I heard Arthur making threats against Elsie. He said he would pay her back for something, but I don't know what."

Throughout this examination, Herbert had been fidgeting nervously, hoping someone else would reveal the truth before the obligation fell on him. But when Mr. Dinsmore asked if anyone knew what Elsie had done to anger Arthur, Herbert dutifully replied. As carefully as he could, he repeated the details of the story he had told his mother that afternoon. As the truth came out, Arthur lost his defiance, and those who watched him could see the fear growing in his eyes and face.

When Herbert finished, Lora Dinsmore stepped forward and handed a scrap of paper to her father. It was a note she had found in the schoolroom — a note written in Arthur's handwriting and promising payment of a debt.

As Mr. Dinsmore read its contents, he groaned. "Has it come to this?" he asked. "My own son — a gambler?" Then he turned to Arthur, and with a hardness in his voice that allowed no protest, he commanded, "Go to your room now, Arthur. You are to remain there in solitary confinement until I have arranged for you to be sent away from my house. Perhaps at boarding school you will learn what it means to be a man of honor. Until you do, you are not worthy to remain with your family."

For once, Arthur obeyed without question.

Elsie's Impossible Choice

Elsie, of course, knew nothing of what was happening in the drawing room. Horace had carried her to her own room after supper and promised to rejoin her there. Chloe, a skillful and tender nurse, had dressed Elsie for bed, being cautious not to cause the child any further pain, and had settled the bandaged ankle on a soft pillow. Elsie was sitting up in bed when her father entered, and her little Bible lay in her hands. Cheerfully, he suggested reading a story together, but he was somewhat surprised when his daughter requested a chapter in the Scriptures.

"I had hoped to read something happier," he said and smiled. "But tonight, your request is my command. Which chapter shall it be?"

Elsie opened her book to the fifty-third chapter of Isaiah, and when her father had read the verses to her, she asked for the twenty-third chapter of Luke. As Horace read, in his fine, clear voice, Elsie closed her eyes and a look of peace seemed to fill her face.

When he finished, Horace asked, "What made you choose this chapter, my dear?

"Because it is all about Jesus and tells us how patiently He bore sorrow and suffering. I want so much to be like Him, Papa. To hear about Him makes it easier for me to forgive and be patient, just as He forgave."

"You're thinking about Arthur," Horace observed accurately. "*I* will find it very hard to forgive him. I know all about what happened and how badly he has treated you." Then he recounted to her everything that had occurred that evening.

Tears welled in Elsie's eyes and tumbled down her cheeks. "I don't understand," she said, "why Arthur hates me so. I've always tried to be kind to him. I had to tell on him once — that time when he blamed Jim for breaking Grandpa's watch. But that was the only time."

Horace put a comforting arm around her. "You no longer have to worry about him, Elsie. He is being sent away to boarding school, so he will have no more opportunities to hurt you."

Elsie stiffened. "Boarding school?" she said with a sharp little cry. "Oh, Papa, that's terrible! I can't think of anything worse than being sent away and having to live with strangers. Can't you ask Grandpa to forgive him this time? Must he be sent away?"

Elsie's reaction surprised Horace, and he tried to reassure her: "It's really for his own good, dear. He needs to learn his lesson, and he will benefit from being away from his mother's spoiling. Besides, I cannot feel safe for you while he is around. I told your grandfather that either Arthur must go to boarding school or you and I must leave for a home of our own."

At his final words, Elsie's face lit up with eagerness. "Is that possible, Papa? Could we have a home of our own someday?"

"Would you like it?"

"Oh, very much. When will it happen, Papa?"

Horace laughed. "Probably not for some time. Perhaps we shall stay here until you are old enough to be my housekeeper," he teased. "Or maybe I should ask Miss Stevens to keep house for us."

"Not that, Papa!" Elsie exclaimed. "Miss Stevens would ruin everything! Besides, I'm sure she is too grand to be anyone's housekeeper."

"Don't be alarmed, dear. I have no intention of ever asking such a thing of Miss Stevens. Now, it's time to say your prayers and get to sleep. It has been a long, wearying day, my little Daughter, and I hope we shall never have another like it."

Horace stayed while Elsie prayed, and he listened carefully to her words. To his amazement, much of what Elsie said concerned Arthur. She asked her Heavenly Father to forgive the boy and guide him through the trials ahead. She asked Him to help Arthur conquer his evil ways. And she asked that Arthur should come to know God's love in his heart.

"Will I never understand my child?" Horace asked himself as he left her room a few moments later. "How can she be so forgiving, when I feel only rage? What is this difference between us?"

But he had no answers. Horace merely shook his head and returned to the guests.

A Slow Recovery

"I have learned the secret of being content in any and every situation."

PHILIPPIANS 4:12

A Slow Recovery

*I*n spite of all that had happened the previous day, the New Year began brightly at Roselands. The servants were full of hustle and bustle as they lit fires in every room, set the dining table for a special breakfast, and carried out the many tasks required by a household greatly enlarged by the presence of so many guests. Though Mrs. Dinsmore had decreed that her guests should be allowed to sleep late during the holidays, the adults and children seemed eager to be dressed and about on this first day of the brand new year. In every room save Arthur's — where the condemned boy, forbidden the company of others, could only lie in his bed and nurse his anger and dread — the stirrings began early, and the sounds of talk and laughter seemed to echo throughout the house.

Everyone, of course, wanted to know about Elsie's health, and the children were especially anxious to see her. Horace, who had already checked on his daughter several times that morning, finally agreed that she could receive visitors after breakfast.

When Horace ushered her friends into her room a little while later, they found Elsie dressed, sitting on her sofa with her bandaged ankle resting on a pillow, and looking as cheerful as if nothing had happened to her. To all the condolences, Elsie replied that she really felt very well and that the doctor had said she would be up and about in just a few weeks. The children were genuinely relieved, for they had been badly frightened by Elsie's fall. They all laughed and talked with great animation.

83

Elsie's Impossible Choice

At length, Horace interrupted the happy babble of young voices. "Elsie," he said, "I have an errand in the city this morning that should take no more than two hours. But since I promised to give you my total attention, I can send someone else if you like. Do you want me here, or can you spare me for a couple of hours? It will be your decision."

Elsie smiled warmly and replied, "I'll miss you, Papa, but I'm sure my friends will keep me busy. You do what's best."

Horace bent down to pat her cheek. "That's my good girl," he said. "I think you will be glad of your decision when I return." Then he turned his smile on the other children. "I can see that you have quite a lot of entertainment here. And I know I can trust your friends not to let you become tired."

A chorus went up: "Yes, sir! We'll take care of her!"

So Horace retreated, stopping to speak to Aunt Chloe, who sat knitting in her chair beside the door. "I leave you in charge," he whispered. "Just don't let her become fatigued."

Horace hardly needed to instruct Chloe, who was as careful a nursemaid as any child could have and had no intention of allowing any harm to come to her dear Elsie. When, about an hour later, she saw that her charge was beginning to look weary, Chloe gently shooed all the children out — all except Herbert Carrington whom Elsie asked to stay.

Herbert, seated in Elsie's rosewood rocking chair, appreciated the opportunity to comfort his friend and help her forget her pain. After all, Elsie had so often done the same for him when he was ill. They talked quietly for a while; then Herbert read from a story book that he knew was a favorite of Elsie's. The time passed so quickly that both youngsters were surprised by Horace's return. Herbert immediately noticed a package in Horace's hand,

and thinking it might be something special for Elsie, the boy asked to be excused.

Elsie also saw the package but was too polite to ask what it contained. Horace, however, lay the bundle in her lap. "This is the cause of my errand," he said. "A New Year's present for my little girl. But before you open it, let me put you on my knee. I'm sure you're tired of sitting in that one spot for so long."

When she was lifted onto her father's lap, Elsie looked at him questioningly.

"Go ahead," Horace smiled. "It's yours to open."

Elsie hurriedly untied the string and stripped away the wrapping paper to reveal a large, beautiful wax doll.

"Papa!" she exclaimed. "It's just like a real baby! A real baby girl! Look at her sweet face. Oh, and her pretty little fingers. And her dress. Oh, I love her already!"

Horace took almost as much pleasure in Elsie's excitement as she did in the new doll. He reached for the package, which had fallen to the floor, and said, "You're not finished yet. There is more at the bottom of this bundle." Then he drew out a pile of cloth remnants — lovely cottons and silks and muslins. "I thought you would enjoy making your doll's clothes yourself," he explained.

"Oh, I shall!" Elsie said. "I shall make her such beautiful new clothes."

Holding the doll firmly in one arm, she wrapped her other around her father's neck. "Thank you so much, Papa! Now I won't mind at all having to stay inside and not being able to play. I'll have so much to do. Papa, what would you think if I name my doll Rose, for Miss Allison?"

"Name her what you like," Horace laughed, "for she is all yours."

"That means I'm her Mamma," Elsie said. Then she giggled, "And you're her grandfather!"

This drew another hearty laugh from Horace, and Elsie went on, "But you need some gray hairs, like other grandfathers. Do you know that Carrie Howard says you look almost too young to be my Papa? She says you look the same age as her brother who has just come home from college. How old are you, Papa?"

"Well, let's see if you can figure that out. You are nine now, and I am eighteen years older. So what is my age?"

Elsie carefully added the numbers in her head. "Twenty-seven," she said with a grin. Then she grew serious. "That is pretty old, I guess. But I'm glad you don't have gray hair and wrinkles, Papa. I'm glad you're young and handsome."

Horace hugged her close, hiding his smile in her curly hair, and said, "And I'm glad you are happy with your doll. I hope it will make up for what happened to your old doll. Mrs. Brown told me how it was broken and that she had mended it. But she said it would never be quite the same, and I wanted you to have a doll you could play with and enjoy."

Elsie glanced at the table beside her bed. Atop it sat the treasured baby doll that had been the gift of her guardian so many years ago. Yes, Mrs. Brown had repaired its broken head, and it looked the same as before. But because of Enna's selfish and careless act, the doll was now very fragile and could no longer be played with. Gazing at her old doll, Elsie hugged her new one tightly. "Now I can love them both, Papa," she said softly. "But I think I will love my new doll just a little better, because she is from you."

Horace had some work to attend to, but before he left Elsie, he sent Chloe to find his daughter's playmates — Carrie, Lucy, and Mary Leslie — to come and join her.

"But don't tell them what I have," Elsie warned her nursemaid. "I want them to be surprised."

After some searching, Chloe finally located the three girls in a small back parlor. They were delighted to receive the invitation because, in truth, they were somewhat at loose ends and missed Elsie's good company. On entering Elsie's room, they immediately saw the new doll, which Elsie held in her lap, and the stack of handsome materials at her side.

"See what Papa has given me," Elsie said. "Will you help me make her new clothes?"

"Oh, yes!" Lucy cried. "I'm so tired of playing all the time that I'd love to sit and sew."

"Me, too!" Mary Leslie chimed. "And I'll be ever so careful not to spoil them."

"Of course, we won't spoil them," Carrie said with a little toss of her head. "I've made more doll clothes than I can count, and it will be such fun to dress your beautiful doll, Elsie."

Chloe provided all the necessary sewing items, and the girls were soon busy making patterns and cutting cloth and stitching tiny seams. Horace left them to their work, under Chloe's watchful eye, and the girls worked happily until the dinner bell rang.

"May we come back this afternoon?" Mary Leslie asked with some concern. "I want to finish this apron, and we are going home tomorrow."

All the girls looked to Chloe. "I'm sure that will be just fine," the nursemaid said, "so long as Miss Elsie has some resting time. Her father wants her to have an hour of quiet after her lunch, so why don't you young ladies return about two o'clock?"

"Please do," Elsie pleaded. "I'm sorry you're going home so soon, Mary Leslie. What about you, Lucy and Carrie? Are you leaving tomorrow?"

"We'll be here till Saturday," said Lucy, "and the Howards, too." Carrie nodded and added, "So we'll be able to make two or three dresses for your Rose before we go."

Most of the Dinsmores' guests did depart the next day, and Roselands suddenly seemed very quiet. Elsie and Lucy and Carrie spent their time together in Elsie's room, completing a handsome new wardrobe for the doll. Herbert and Harry often joined them and took turns reading aloud, to everyone's enjoyment. And so the remainder of the holidays passed peacefully until the Howards and the Carringtons left on Saturday. It was only when they had all said their good-byes that Elsie realized how much she would miss the company of her dear friends.

She felt her confinement even more on Sunday, when she could not attend church. Her father offered to stay at home, but Elsie begged him to go to services without her. They would, after all, have the afternoon and evening to spend together.

That evening, they shared what had become a very special time for Elsie — reading the Bible and singing hymns in the waning hours of the Sabbath. Elsie loved to sing with her father, her sweet voice blending with his deep bass. She talked with him about what she read in the Bible, asking him occasional questions which he was, even with all his learning and experience, scarcely capable of answering.

At last, she settled into his lap, her head resting against his shoulder, and was silent. He could tell that she was not sleeping and wondered about her thoughts. At length, he broke into her reverie by asking, "What are you thinking about, Daughter?"

"I was thinking about Arthur, Papa. I would like very much to give him a nice present before he goes away. May I?"

"If you wish," Horace replied.

"Thank you, Papa. I was half-afraid you wouldn't let me. Since I can't go shopping, will you buy the present for me the next time you go into the city? I'd like to give him the very best pocket Bible you can find. And I'd like for you to write his name inside, and mine, so he'll know it is a token of affection from me. Will you, Papa?"

"I will, dear, but I doubt Arthur will appreciate such a gift," Horace said gently.

"He might, Papa, if it is *very* handsomely bound," Elsie said, though her voice betrayed her own doubts. "I want to try anyway. When does Arthur leave, Papa?"

"The day after tomorrow."

"Do you think he might come and see me before he goes? I wish he would."

"I'll ask him," Horace promised. "But why do you want to see him after all the pain he has caused you?"

Elsie sighed deeply. "I want him to know that I'm not angry with him and that I feel so sorry he has to go away all alone to live with strangers."

By now, Horace was used to Elsie's ability to forgive, but her sympathy for Arthur still took him by surprise. "You need not waste your kind thoughts on him," Horace said a little hotly. "In fact, I think he rather likes the idea of going away to school."

Elsie's Impossible Choice

Now it was Elsie's turn to be surprised, for nothing could frighten her more than the thought of being separated from her Papa. "He does?" she exclaimed. "How strange!"

True to his form, Arthur did refuse to see Elsie and even wanted to decline her gift. But when Lora suggested that he might need a Bible for his schoolwork and when he saw that the little book was indeed very handsome, he grudgingly accepted the present. But nothing could convince him to see Elsie, and when she sent him a gracious little note, he ignored her offer of friendship. And so Arthur departed from Roselands without any apology or even a sign that he regretted his behavior.

Miss Day, the governess, had returned from her visit to the North, and soon the children of Roselands were settled again into their usual routines. Elsie could not attend classes in the schoolroom, for her ankle was still very weak, and her father did not press her to take up her studies. But Elsie herself soon became bored with so little to do and found herself wishing to get back to her books.

"Papa?" she asked one morning after breakfast. "Except for my ankle, I'm quite well enough to do my lessons now. Would you let me recite them to you?"

"Certainly, Daughter," Horace replied with some pleasure. "It would be no trouble for me. On the contrary, there's nothing I enjoy more than being your teacher — if you promise to be a diligent student."

Elsie promised faithfully, and from that morning on, she pursued her studies as regularly as if she were in class. Still, she looked forward to the day when she would no longer be confined to the house, when she could take walks again and ride her pony in the fresh air. But she wasn't often lonely; her father spent all his spare time with her, and when he could not be there, others took his place. Edward Travilla often stopped by for a visit, and he always brought Elsie a treat — beautiful bouquets or fresh fruits from his hothouse or something delicious from his mother's kitchen or best of all, a new book. Adelaide and Lora came to her room every day to talk and tell her what was happening in the household. Several times, Walter brought his books and asked for Elsie's help with his lessons. Then they would talk, and he told her how much he regretted her injury and missed her presence in the schoolroom.

Her new doll was another source of comfort. Elsie loved it dearly and was extremely careful of it, fearing to let anyone but herself handle it. It was especially annoying when Enna asked to hold the doll. Elsie knew from experience how dangerous it was to deny any wish of Enna's unless Horace was there, so she tried to keep the doll out of sight whenever Enna was around.

But one afternoon, Enna burst into her room without knocking, just as Elsie was dressing her doll in one of its new outfits.

"She's so pretty!" Enna cried. "Let me take her on my lap for a little while. I won't hurt her."

Elsie tried not to give in, but when Enna began to whine, she relented. "Just for a minute, and you must be very careful," she warned. "You know that if she falls, she will surely break."

Enna pulled the little rocking chair close to Elsie's couch, took the baby doll in her arms, and sat down. Enna seemed quite conscientious at first, but Elsie could only watch her nervously and wish that Aunt Chloe, who had gone to the kitchen, would come back quickly.

Not content to rock the doll and sing to her, Enna was soon busy unfastening the clothes and removing the shoes and stockings so she could see the doll's feet. Elsie watched in helpless terror as Enna rocked faster and faster. Little pieces of clothing seemed to fly everywhere. When the baby shoes slipped from her knee to the floor, Enna jumped up to get them, and the doll sprang from her lap into the air. Without a thought, Elsie rushed off the couch and caught the doll before it could shatter, but the movement caused Elsie to twist her ankle badly, and she fell onto the floor, almost fainting from the pain. Seeing Elsie's pale face, Enna ran from the room.

A few moments later, Horace entered to find his daughter crumpled on the floor and grasping her ankle. Rushing to her, he saw the tears running down her terribly white face.

"What has happened?" he asked in fright and alarm.

"Oh, Papa," Elsie sobbed. "Enna dropped my doll, and I jumped up and caught it and hurt my ankle."

"What did you do that for?" he demanded angrily. "No doll is worth having you crippled!"

"Please don't be mad, Papa!" Elsie begged between her sobs. "I didn't have time to think, and I'll never do it again!"

Horace was too busy checking the ankle to reply, and when Chloe came in, he was lifting Elsie onto her bed. Seeing the nursemaid, he harshly scolded her for leaving his child alone. Chloe, who could see how much Elsie was suffering, didn't say a word but instantly went to help Horace. In not too many minutes, Elsie's tears had stopped, and the color had come back to her face.

"Are you better now, darling?" Chloe asked.

"Yes, Aunt Chloe. The pain is almost gone," Elsie replied, although she was looking not at her nurse, but into her father's face.

"I'm not angry with you," he said as he gently smoothed back her curls and kissed her cheek. "Nor with Aunt Chloe. I was only angry that my dear child should be hurt again for the sake of a toy."

There was, however, one who had earned Horace's full wrath, and as soon as Elsie was comfortable, he left her in Chloe's care and sought out his father and stepmother. In the strongest words possible, he demanded that Enna never again enter Elsie's room unless he was present. Old Mr. Dinsmore promptly agreed and did not give his wife even a second to protest. But in her heart, she marked up yet another grievance against her stepson's daughter. "Her day will come," Mrs. Dinsmore thought darkly to herself. "Yes, the time will come when that little upstart child will pay for every unhappiness she has caused my own poor children."

CHAPTER

6

A Clash
of Wills

*"Remember the Sabbath day
by keeping it holy."*

EXODUS 20:8

*I*n spite of the second injury to her ankle, Elsie made quick progress under her Papa's cautious and loving care — and she was soon again following her accustomed routines. She joined the other children in the schoolroom, and although Miss Day was hardly so devoted or knowledgeable a teacher as Horace, classes were more comfortable now that Arthur was away. Without his constant teasing and harassing, all the children were better able to concentrate on their lessons. Even Miss Day seemed less inclined to find fault with her pupils, and Elsie gave the governess no excuses for complaint. Elsie continued her daily hour of study with her father, and when the weather began to warm, Horace took her for walks and carriage rides, and he supervised her return to pony riding, making sure that nothing should jeopardize her full recovery.

Elsie was happiest of all when she was allowed to attend church services again. For as long as she could remember, Elsie had honored the Sabbath as the most sacred day of each week — for it was the day God had set aside for the faithful to rest from their labors, honor Him, gather with others in worship, study His Holy Word, and learn more about the meaning and the greatness of His forgiving love. Long before she had come to Roselands or met her father, Elsie had been raised to believe in absolute obedience to all of God's commandments. Mrs. Murray, the Scottish housekeeper who was Elsie's first teacher and caretaker so many years ago in New Orleans, had particularly stressed the importance of the Fourth Commandment's requirement to keep the Sabbath day holy. So for Elsie — if for few others in the Dinsmore household — the Sabbath was the day to put aside all earthly concerns and personal indulgences and to do only those things that would honor and glorify God.

In the past, Elsie's strict observation of the Sabbath had frequently brought her into conflict with other members of her family, even her dear Papa. But, though Horace was sometimes angered by Elsie's unbending principles on the Sabbath when they clashed with his own will, many months had passed without any quarrels. In fact, Elsie's greatest fear — that her father might someday force her to choose between his commands and God's commandments — had almost faded away.

Except for Lora, who was struggling in her own way to become a devoted Christian, the Dinsmores attended Sunday services merely as a matter of form. They all enjoyed dressing up and taking the weekly carriage ride into the city and seeing their friends and neighbors. Unlike Elsie, they took little notice of the minister's words or the lessons of the week. Although Horace seemed to respect his daughter's wishes — reading and discussing the Bible with her and sometimes joining her in hymn-singing — Sundays at Roselands were for the most part days devoted to playing and entertaining guests, not set aside for rest and spiritual contemplation. Elsie truly loved the Lord, who had been both loving Father and Best Friend to her for so many years, and it saddened the little girl that her family did not understand the importance of God's commandments. But her own resolve to do His will never wavered.

It was on a Sunday morning in the early days of spring that Elsie's greatest trial began, but neither she nor anyone else in all of Roselands had any suspicion of what lay ahead.

Elsie had risen, read her Bible and said her prayers, and been carefully dressed by Aunt Chloe. Outside her window, the trees were still bare, but the brown of the lawns was rapidly being replaced by the bright green of spring grass, and the yellow heads of the early daffodils seemed to bow and wave at Elsie in the soft morning breeze. The sky was a light, hazy blue but cloudless, and Elsie, who was learning from her father to observe nature's signs, thought that it would be a beautiful day.

A few minutes later, she was knocking at Horace's door, ready to join him for their morning walk before breakfast. But the voice that bid her to enter did not carry its usual strong tone, and as soon as Elsie opened the door, she knew that something was wrong. Instead of greeting her with hugs and heartiness, Horace lay stretched out on his sofa. He was dressed, but in place of his neat wool jacket, he wore his dressing gown over his shirt, and a soft coverlet drifted across his legs. Despite his effort to smile, his face was flushed and pained.

"Dear Papa, are you sick?" Elsie asked, rushing to his side.

"I believe I am, Daughter. I have a terrible headache, and I feel hot and chilled at the same time," he replied. "But don't be worried, dear. It's nothing serious, I'm sure. Just a little springtime cold. That's all."

His words were reassuring, but Elsie could plainly see that he was ill. "Can I be your nurse, Papa?" she asked. "Would you like some water and a cloth for your head?"

"That would be fine, my dear," he replied, smiling a bit more brightly.

Elsie left the room, but she returned almost immediately, followed by Chloe who carried a pitcher of cold water. The woman and the little girl set about making Horace as comfortable as they could. Chloe fetched a basin of water and a small towel from the dressing room and prepared a soft, damp cloth for Horace's fevered forehead. Then she closed the curtains to darken the room and set about straightening the bedclothes and fluffing the pillows in hopes of convincing Horace to return to his comfortable bed. Elsie poured cold water into a small tumbler and held it for her father to drink.

"Shouldn't we send for Doctor Barton?" she asked anxiously.

"I hardly think that's necessary," Horace responded.

But Chloe, who had nursed many patients through illnesses both mild and serious, said, "It can't hurt you to call the doctor in, Mr. Horace. It can't hurt a bit, and it might do a world of good."

"Yes, Papa," Elsie added. "Doctor Barton can only do you good."

Horace was in no mood to argue, so he merely sighed and said, "If it pleases you, then send for the good doctor — though I'm afraid he will think us silly for making a fuss over a little cold."

Leaving Elsie to watch over her father, Chloe went to find young Jim, the stable boy. He was in the kitchen, preparing to eat his breakfast; on hearing Chloe's message, however, he lingered only long enough to grab a hot biscuit and his rough coat. Then he was off to saddle a fast horse and ride to town in search of the doctor.

Meanwhile, Elsie was keeping careful watch over her Papa as he drifted in and out of sleep. Even her young eyes could clearly see the pain in his face. She bathed his hot forehead with the cool, damp cloth and tried to keep the coverlet wrapped about him, even when he tried to push it away.

Horace managed a smile for her every now and then. "That cloth does soothe my aching head," he said softly. "Where did you learn to be so good a nurse, dear Daughter?"

"I sometimes have bad headaches myself," Elsie explained, "and I know how Aunt Chloe cares for me."

"You are a very good pupil," Horace observed and closed his eyes. Despite her worry about her father's health, Elsie felt a flush of pleasure at his compliment.

And so they remained — the father finally seeming to sleep; the daughter watching his face for any sign of change.

Not too many minutes later, Chloe returned just as the breakfast bell was ringing. The sound roused Horace. "You must go down to breakfast now," he instructed Elsie. She started to protest, but before a word could escape her mouth, he said, "No argument, Elsie. You must eat a good breakfast for your own strength, and then you must prepare for church."

"But, Papa —"

Horace cut her off. "I want you to go to church, Elsie. Your Aunt Adelaide will watch over you today, and Chloe will take good care of me until you return."

"I'll do that, Mr. Horace," Chloe said with a confident smile. And to Elsie she added, "You know you can trust me, child."

Elsie knew it was useless to beg and would only upset her father. So she kissed him once more and left to do his bidding.

Elsie's Impossible Choice

Still, she hardly tasted her breakfast that morning and heard barely a word of the minister's Sunday sermon, for her mind was elsewhere. She had never before known her father to be ill, and deep inside her, the possibility of losing him arose like a dark and fearsome cloud.

When the family at long last arrived back at Roselands, Elsie was the first to spot Doctor Barton's black buggy in the drive. The doctor was just coming out of the front door, and as soon as the Dinsmores' carriage came to a stop, Elsie jumped down — forgetting all about her ankle — and ran to him.

His face stern, but with a twinkle in his eye, Doctor Barton said, "Slow down, young Elsie, or I will be bandaging that leg of yours again."

"I'm fine, Doctor Barton, but my Papa —" Elsie said.

"Well, he's not as fine as you, my dear, but I don't believe his condition is serious. If he stays quiet and takes the medicine I have left, he should be right in a week or two."

"Are you sure, sir?" Elsie asked.

"As sure as anyone can be," the doctor said with a cheerful wink. "I have left instructions for his care with Chloe, and I shall speak with Mrs. Dinsmore before I go. And your father tells me that you are an excellent nurse — he could ask for no better. May I tell you what you can do for him?"

"Oh yes, sir!" Elsie exclaimed, immensely pleased that the doctor would trust her with such responsibility.

"Good. I am depending on you to see that your father follows my orders and takes his medicine. And on no account should he become over-excited until he is completely well again. It's important that he not be upset by anything. Can you see to that, Elsie?" the doctor asked in his gravest tone.

"Oh, I will, Doctor Barton," Elsie pledged. "I promise."

"Then I will leave him in your care," the kindly doctor said, and he turned to address Mr. and Mrs. Dinsmore as Elsie hurried inside and — not even stopping to remove her coat — upstairs to her father's room. Opening the door without a sound, she saw that her father had moved from the sofa to the bed. Not far from his side, Aunt Chloe sat in a comfortable rocking chair. Sensing Elsie's presence, the nursemaid smiled and put her finger to her lips. As Elsie approached the bed, she could see that her Papa was sleeping soundly and that his face no longer bore the flush that had frightened her so that morning.

"Your Papa's going to be just fine," Chloe said in the softest whisper. "Now, you go take off your coat and hat, child, and then go on down to dinner. After you eat, you can take my place sitting with him."

Elsie didn't say a word for fear of waking her father, but after checking his sleeping face once more, she tiptoed from the room.

Indeed, Horace did seem to improve with the passage of each new day, although he continued to suffer from the headaches and the fever never entirely left him. Under Mrs. Dinsmore's strict supervision, Chloe saw that the doctor's orders were carried out to the letter. And over Mrs. Dinsmore's strenuous objections (for the woman disapproved of any children in a sickroom), Elsie spent every spare minute with Horace. Her mere presence seemed to do him good; watching her go about her "nursing" chores — keeping his water glass filled, preparing cool cloths for his head, fluffing his pillows, and doing everything in her small power to make him comfortable — seemed to lighten his heart. It was tedious for an active man like Horace to be confined to bed, and her attentions greatly relieved his boredom. For her part, Elsie would have spent all her waking hours at his beck and call, but Horace was adamant that she follow her normal routine. So she attended her classes in the schoolroom, took her meals with the family, and never missed her morning walks in the garden and afternoon rides with Jim as her watchful companion.

What Horace enjoyed most was Elsie's reading. His illness had made his eyes quite sensitive, and he could not focus on a book page for long. So he quickly came to depend on Elsie to read aloud to him, and he tried to choose books and stories that they could enjoy together. Elsie also learned to read the newspapers which Horace counted on for news of business and politics; although she understood little of the events she read about, she didn't mind because the papers were so important to her father.

And so, by the following Sunday, Horace was feeling a good deal better, though he was not yet well. Returning from church, Elsie had been allowed to have her dinner on a tray in her father's room. Afterwards, while Chloe was clearing the trays and administering Horace's medicine, Elsie retrieved her little Bible from her room; she wanted to read for her father the fifth chapter of Acts, which had been the subject of that morning's church lesson.

Horace indulged her wish, but he was restless and peevish — as people in the last stages of an illness often are — and barely heard a word Elsie read. He even missed the most important verse, when Peter and the apostles reply to the High Priest of the Sanhedrin, "We must obey God rather than men!" Oh, if only Horace had opened his heart to those words.

Elsie finished the chapter and was preparing to read the next when Horace stopped her.

"No more Bible reading, Daughter," he said. "I am in no mood today. Get that newspaper from my desk, dear. I'd like you to read it to me."

Poor Elsie — this was the moment she had dreaded for so long. She knew that articles in the newspaper, whatever their content, were not about God and His ways; she knew they would be unfit for Sabbath reading. Yet her father's command was clear. She hesitated, trying to think what to do. Then she moved slowly to the desk where the newspaper lay.

"What are you waiting for?" Horace asked, a tone of impatience clear in his voice. "Bring the paper here now."

Elsie took it and returned to his bedside. It was then that Horace realized something was wrong. "Tears, Elsie?" he asked. "What ails you child? Are you ill?"

His voice was now full of tender concern, and Elsie lay her head against his shoulder. "Oh, Papa," she managed to say, "You know I want to do whatever you ask, but I cannot read that newspaper today. Please, Papa, not on the Sabbath!"

Horace did not reply at first, and for a moment, Elsie hoped that he had reconsidered. But then he spoke, and his voice was more stern and cold than she had heard it in many months.

"I do not ask. I *command* you to read that paper. And what's more, I intend to be obeyed *now*. Sit down at once and begin. I want no more of this behavior."

"Papa," she said tearfully, "I *never* want to disobey you. But I must not break the Sabbath. Please, let me read you something suitable, and I'll read this newspaper first thing tomorrow."

Elsie's Impossible Choice

Horace gently raised her head from his shoulder and looked into her tear-streaked face. In a tone less harsh but still full of determination, he said: "I had hoped you learned a better lesson from the event of last spring." (Elsie well remembered the terrible day almost a year before, when she had refused to sing a popular song for his guests on the Sabbath.)

"I see now that you think you may do as you like in these matters," Horace continued. "But you are mistaken. I would never ask you to do anything wrong, but I can see no harm in reading that newspaper today. And I am much more capable of judging these matters than you are. Why, I have often seen ministers reading their newspapers on the Sabbath. Surely what is good for them is good enough for you."

Timidly, Elsie responded, "But aren't we supposed to do whatever God tells us without asking what other people do, Papa? Don't very good people sometimes do wrong?"

Growing tired, Horace sank back on his pillow and directed, "Find me a text that says you are not to read a newspaper on Sunday, and I will let you wait until tomorrow."

Elsie thought for some moments. "I can't find one that says just that, Papa," Elsie began slowly, "but the Fourth Commandment says we should keep the Sabbath day holy. In the book of Isaiah, it says we are not to do as we please or go our own way or speak idle words on the Sabbath. Doesn't that mean it is wrong to read worldly thoughts and words on the Sabbath?"

Exasperated, Horace exclaimed, "Nonsense! You are far too young to understand such subjects. Your duty is to obey me. Are you going to read that newspaper?"

Elsie was distraught. She did not want to be disobedient; she wanted always to please her father. But she had a higher duty. "I cannot read it, Papa," she said in a small whisper. "I just can't."

There was a long silence, as Elsie struggled to hold her tears back. Finally her father spoke, in a calm voice that somehow frightened her more than his former sternness. "Then until you are ready to obey," he said, leaning forward and gently touching her head, "I do not want you with me. I will not have the company of a disobedient daughter. You have ten minutes to make your choice, Elsie. Obedience or banishment from my sight. If you choose not to obey me, then you must leave my room and not return until you are ready to acknowledge your fault."

At the thought of being separated from her dear Papa, Elsie burst into sobs, for she could not contain her misery. Horace turned away from her and took up his pocket watch, which lay on the bedside table. He was confident that she would submit, but as the minutes slowly ticked by — one, two, three, four — Elsie said nothing. Her tears flowed. Her turmoil was great. But believing that she was being asked to choose between her earthly father and her Heavenly Father, Elsie knew there could be only one answer.

In her heart, she uttered a desperate prayer for the help of God's Holy Spirit. Instantly, Jesus' words from the book of Matthew came to her: "Love the Lord your God with all your heart and with all your soul and with all your strength. This is the first and greatest commandment."

When the ten minutes had gone by, Horace said, "The time is up. What is your decision?"

In a voice more full of sadness than Horace had ever heard before, she replied, "I cannot read the newspaper, Papa. Not on the Sabbath."

Elsie's Impossible Choice

Horace looked into her face and was tempted for an instant to retreat. But on the outcome of this battle, he truly believed, rested his entire control over his child. If Elsie were allowed to defy his authority now, what might happen to her in the future? The image of his brother Arthur flashed before him, and his heart hardened. Elsie must not be allowed to follow that path.

"My dear, this separation will be as painful for me as for you," he said truthfully, "but I cannot tolerate disobedience from my child. So let me ask you once more. Will you obey?"

Elsie, her throat choked with tears, knew that more words were useless. She lowered her head and said nothing.

"Then go," Horace said in a flat tone. "Send one of the servants to care for me, but you are not to return until you are ready to comply with my conditions. Do you understand?"

Elsie nodded, and without a word she crossed to the door and left her father's room.

When she had gone, Horace collapsed back onto his bed. He suddenly felt worse than he had in days, but he comforted himself with these thoughts: "She has some of my own obstinacy in her character, but a few days of banishment will bring her around. I know it will. It is a hard punishment for us both, for I shall miss her presence deeply. But it is for her own good. Definitely, for her own good."

CHAPTER

7

At Death's Door

*"Be merciful to me Lord,
for I am faint . . . .
My soul is in anguish."*

PSALM 6:2-3

fter summoning a servant for her father, Elsie ran to her room, shut the door, and threw herself upon the bed. She gave way totally to her grief, weeping bitterly at her terrible punishment. The separation from her father was all the harder to bear because she knew in her heart that he was acting not from cruel motives, but from a genuine, if misguided, sense of duty to her.

Outside, the day was as beautiful as Elsie had predicted it would be, but no sunlight could penetrate her misery. Though her sobbing gradually subsided, she could find no relief from the enormous weight that seemed to be crushing down upon her. He had said it was her choice, and she had wanted to cry out, "But there is no choice, Papa! Between God's commands and man's — even yours, Papa — there can never be any choice!" If only he believed as she did . . . if only he knew Jesus as his Savior and Lord . . . if only he understood God's love and great sacrifice . . . if only —

Elsie had lain on her bed for about an hour when Chloe entered. Immediately the nursemaid perceived the child's distress and rushed to her side.

"What is it, child? What troubles you so?" she asked as she raised Elsie tenderly and cradled her.

Elsie gasped out the story, and Chloe immediately understood. She had known this day would eventually come, and now she strove to comfort the child without casting blame on the father. In the most soothing tones, she assured Elsie of her own unalterable affection and talked of the love of Jesus. He would help Elsie through this trial, Chloe said, and would remove it in His own time.

Elsie's Impossible Choice

Elsie grew calmer as she listened to her nursemaid's words. She allowed Chloe to bathe her face and smooth her hair and clothing. But she would not leave her room, and indeed, she barely stirred from Chloe's side. The sun, meanwhile, began its slow decline in the sky; and at last, Chloe rose to stoke the fire and light the candles. When the supper bell rang, Chloe exerted all her persuasive abilities to convince Elsie to join the family in the dining room. Although Elsie had no desire for food, she went, in large measure because she knew that her father would expect her to.

Unfortunately, word of her punishment had already reached the other members of the family. Mrs. Dinsmore had gone to Horace's room shortly after Elsie's departure and learned of his distress (though Horace had been careful not to explain the nature of the conflict). Because she never missed an opportunity to belittle Horace's child, Mrs. Dinsmore quickly spread the word of Elsie's disgrace, so when Elsie entered the dining room, she was greeted by cold stares. Even Adelaide and Lora, who both loved their little niece dearly, averted their eyes, for neither could believe that Horace would punish his daughter so severely without good reason.

Before Elsie could take her seat, Enna exclaimed in her most hateful voice, "Bad Elsie! Brother Horace ought to spank you good!"

"And so he should," added Mrs. Dinsmore, "if only he had the strength. But I fear he is unlikely ever to regain his health if he must worry so about his disobedient daughter."

Adelaide, surprised by her mother's sudden concern for Horace, cast a wondering glance at the older woman. But no more words were spoken to Elsie throughout the long and uncomfortable meal. Elsie hardly noticed the others, however, for Mrs. Dinsmore's remark had given her a new fear. Was her father worse?

Indeed, Horace's fever had returned, and his illness had revived alarmingly that afternoon. The conflict with Elsie had upset him terribly, and just the thought of banishing her from his sight had added greatly to his worry. Besides, almost from the moment he dictated her punishment, Horace had doubted the rightness and justice of his action. He was torn. On the one hand, Horace was a man of great pride and indomitable will. He believed that his authority over his child must be absolute if he was to protect her from life's trials and troubles. On the other hand, his love for Elsie was total. In their short time together, she had become the center of his life, and her happiness was his first desire. When Elsie had opposed his command, he found himself caught. A fierce struggle raged inside him all that afternoon, undoing his recovery and plunging him back into fever and pain.

As soon as Elsie was excused from the supper table, she stole into the garden to be alone with her grief and to raise her prayers for her father to God. She was sitting on a bench in her favorite place when she heard the sound of a galloping horse, followed by several excited voices among which she recognized her step-grandmother's and Doctor Barton's. She knew that the doctor must have been called for her father, and her first impulse was to rush to Horace's room. But that would be disobeying and might make his condition even worse. What was she to do?

At length, she heard again the voice of Doctor Barton, and she ran to the house, hoping to speak to him before he departed. But when she reached the portico, the doctor was already far down the driveway, and Elsie could see no more of him than the dust cloud raised by his horse's galloping hooves.

⁓

Drawn by feelings she could not control, Elsie ran to her father's room. She knew she could not enter, but she had to be close to him now. Perhaps someone would pass by and give her news. Perhaps one of the servants would tell her what she wanted so desperately to hear — that Horace was better and would soon be his old self again.

Her own head was throbbing; her eyes were swollen from the many tears she had shed since her last bitter meeting with her father; and she shivered as the cold night air crept through the hall. But Elsie barely noticed her own discomfort as she stationed herself, like a valiant guardian, in the hallway outside Horace's closed door. She could hear activity inside and thought she could make out the voices of Mrs. Dinsmore and Adelaide.

After what seemed a very long time, the door opened, and in the light from Horace's fireplace, a woman's shadowy figure emerged. Elsie's heart leaped, for she thought it was Adelaide. But Mrs. Dinsmore exited, and the woman spotted Elsie before the little girl could recognize her stepgrandmother.

Pulling the door closed behind her, Mrs. Dinsmore demanded in a low, hissing voice, "What are you doing here, Elsie? Have you come to cause your poor father more grief?"

Elsie was too frightened to reply, and the woman went on. "At least you are sufficiently ashamed of yourself not to talk back. But you are responsible for this, you terrible child. Your father is much worse, and Doctor Barton fears for his life. If you are left an orphan, you can thank your own stubborn disobedience for your loss."

Mrs. Dinsmore's final words cut like a knife; for the first time, Elsie realized that her father's very existence was in jeopardy. She had worried about his health and prayed for his recovery, but she had not until this moment considered that he might be taken from her altogether. The thought was unbearable, and Elsie felt fear bursting inside her as Mrs. Dinsmore swept past with a disgusted "Humph" and hurried away down the hall. Thinking she might collapse, Elsie grasped the arm of a chair to steady herself. She stood without moving, like a stone statue. But her mind raced; thoughts and images spun in her head, too jumbled and confused to make any sense. Only one thought came through clearly: "Don't let my Papa die! Please, don't let my Papa die!"

Elsie didn't see or hear her Aunt Adelaide come from Horace's room. Only when a warm hand touched her face did the little girl come back to the moment.

"You're as cold as ice!" Adelaide was exclaiming.

Suddenly Elsie felt as if every bone in her body had turned to jelly. Her hand slipped from the chair arm, and if Adelaide had not grabbed her, Elsie would have collapsed on the floor.

"Dear child," Adelaide said, holding Elsie upright with a firm arm around her waist, "you must go to your room and lie down."

As Adelaide led her away from the closed door, Elsie managed to ask, "Is my Papa dead?"

"No, child, but he is very ill. This setback is severe, and he has little strength to fight it. So you must take care of yourself, Elsie. We don't want to nurse you while your father needs us so much."

Her arm still supporting Elsie's small body, Adelaide guided the child to her room and knocked at the door. Chloe opened it and instantly took Elsie into her grasp.

"Watch her carefully, Aunt Chloe," Adelaide instructed. "I have things to do for Horace, and right now he must be the center of our concerns."

Chloe nodded, for she was well aware how serious Horace's condition had become. With a faint and worried smile, Adelaide left.

"Will my Papa die?" Elsie sobbed. "Will he die?"

Chloe lifted her little charge onto the bed and sat down beside her, enfolding Elsie in her strong and loving embrace.

"He's very ill," Chloe began, "but I think the good Lord will spare him if we pray."

Elsie's pale face was suddenly flushed with color, and warmth seemed to flow through her again. "Oh, yes, yes!" she cried. "We must pray together, Aunt Chloe, and I'm sure God will save Papa. Doesn't He *promise* to grant whatever two ask for in agreement with each other?"

"He does, sweet child. Yes, indeed He does."

And so Elsie and her nursemaid turned to God. They knelt together by the bed, and first Chloe, then Elsie opened their hearts to Jesus, their merciful and compassionate Lord. As her words came out, Elsie felt better. Her burden was not lessened, but now that she was sharing it with the Lord, she felt new hope.

When her fervent prayer was ended, Elsie climbed onto her bed and closed her eyes. With one more silent thought for her Papa, she fell into a deep and peaceful sleep.

Horace's night, however, was anything but peaceful. His fever had risen again, and the medication left by Doctor Barton seemed to provide little relief. Horace drifted in and out of consciousness, and both Adelaide and Mrs. Dinsmore — aided by Horace's servant, John — struggled to keep the sick man as comfortable as possible while they watched for even the smallest change in his condition.

When morning came, Horace at last fell into an exhausted sleep, and Adelaide took advantage of the moment to freshen herself and eat breakfast before going back to the sickroom. The break helped revive her after the long and sleepless night, but Adelaide was extremely worried about her brother. As she left the dining room, she caught sight of Elsie, who sat alone in the library. Adelaide entered and said in a tone that was much sharper than normal, "Elsie, your father is still very bad, and Doctor Barton believes that *something* is troubling his mind. Whatever it is, the doctor believes it is the cause of this alarming illness, and unless the worry is removed, Horace may never be any better. Elsie, *you know what that something is*, and I think that *only you can remove it*."

Adelaide didn't wait for a reply, but her dreadful pronouncement left Elsie shocked and bewildered. What could she do? Certainly not betray her Heavenly Father. But if her Papa died . . .

A new and horrible thought struck her. What if her father died before he had learned to love Jesus? What if he died before he was prepared to go to heaven? The possibility of losing her father in this world was almost too much to bear, but it was nothing when compared to the prospect of not meeting him in eternity.

Elsie's Impossible Choice

Forbidden admission to her father's room by Mrs. Dinsmore and abandoned by the other Dinsmores, Elsie could only pass that long and frightful day in miserable solitude. Chloe, who had been called in to help with the nursing, would bring word of Horace when she could slip away for a few moments. Though the nursemaid tried to sound hopeful, Elsie could see the sadness in her eyes. Toward evening Doctor Barton arrived, and from her seat in the library, Elsie saw him rush toward the stairs that led to her father's room; he did not stop even to remove his coat and hat. It was not long before she heard a servant summoning old Mr. Dinsmore and the rest of the family to come and see Horace — for one last time. But no one came for Elsie.

When she could stand it no longer, Elsie ran upstairs, intending to beg to see her father. She hoped to find Adelaide or perhaps her grandfather — they would not be so cruel as to keep her from her Papa. Instead, Mrs. Dinsmore sat alone in the hall chair outside Horace's door. She was very tired, and fatigue had not softened her feelings.

With no effort to plan her speech, Elsie simply burst out her heart-rending request. "Please, Mrs. Dinsmore," she cried, "I *must* see my Papa! I must tell him how much I love him."

The woman did not move a muscle, but her dark eyes flashed. "Love him?" she retorted. "If you loved him, you would have complied with his wishes. No, you shall not see him until you do as he has commanded you."

"But —"

"There can be no 'but,' you selfish and disobedient girl. Your father has said that you are banished from his sight

118

until you obey him, and I will not go against his wishes. You shall not enter his room."

"But if he dies —"

Mrs. Dinsmore straightened in the chair, and her eyes, now black as night and cold as ice, seemed to bore into the child.

"If he dies," she said, repeating each word with slow contempt, "then his death will be your fault. Now go away. I have no pity to waste on you."

Elsie knew there was no hope left. Mrs. Dinsmore could not — would not — be moved. This woman may as well have been a prison wall that barred Elsie from one last look at her father's face, one last touch of his hand. All she could do now was to pray, and to contemplate her life without mother or father.

CHAPTER 8

A False Witness

"A truthful witness does not deceive, but a false witness pours out lies."

PROVERBS 14:5

*E*lsie, darling. Wake up now."

Elsie heard her name as if it came from a dream. For several moments, she hung between sleep and waking, but when she heard herself called again, she opened her eyes and looked into the face of her nursemaid. Chloe was smiling. No, Chloe was grinning!

"Wake up now, child, for it's a glorious day," the nursemaid said.

"It is? What's happened, Aunt Chloe? Is Papa better?"

"He sure enough is, child. His fever broke last night, and the doctor says he's going to get well for certain, if he doesn't get worse again."

"Is it true, Aunt Chloe? Really true?"

"Have I ever told you anything but the truth?" Chloe laughed.

"Oh, God is so good!" Elsie exclaimed as tears of gratitude and relief filled her bright eyes. "He has answered our prayers!"

And for a while, as the wonderful news of her father's recovery danced in her head, Elsie experienced the pure, sweet joy that comes from knowing that God in His great mercy has preserved a dearly loved one from harm. All her thoughts were for her father and his return from the edge of death. Then a shadow fell over her as she remembered her own situation — disgraced and banished from her dear Papa's company. Could that ever be cured?

Elsie's Impossible Choice

Horace's recovery went very slowly, for his illness had weakened him seriously. He kept to his bed for several weeks, tended by Mrs. Dinsmore and her servants. All of Elsie's requests to see him had been denied, so on the morning that he at last came downstairs to join the family at breakfast, she was shocked at his appearance. Her robust and handsome Papa was so altered — pale, thin, and sad-eyed.

At the sight of him, Elsie felt her heart would break. As the rest of the family surrounded him, pouring out their congratulations and good wishes, Elsie longed to run into his arms and feel his embrace once more. But she could not. Watching as Enna received a smile and a gentle kiss from Horace, Elsie felt as if time had turned backwards and she was once again the lonely little girl of a year ago, afraid to approach her newly returned parent for fear he did not love her. But her pain was all the greater now because she had learned to love him with all her heart and to count on his deep love in return. Before she met Horace, he had been a dream, an ideal only; now he was a real father to her, and the possibility of losing his affection forever was too much to bear.

Sitting across the table from him, she felt hot tears gathering in her eyes, but she struggled with all her might to hold them back. Her Papa had so often complained that her tears flowed too easily; she could not disappoint him by crying now. She kept her eyes on her plate, choked down her bread and milk, and said nothing. No one seemed to notice her, and not once did Horace glance in her direction (although, in truth, he was more aware of her presence than of anyone else's). When the meal ended, Elsie managed to slip away to her room.

 124

Just after Christmas, Edward Travilla had given Elsie a lovely and rare plant from his hothouse. He had shown her how to care for it and promised that if she kept it properly watered, the plant would produce beautiful blooms. Elsie had tended the plant according to Mr. Travilla's instructions, and as it happened, the first buds had opened the day before. Now she gazed at the fragile white flowers, catching their sweet fragrance, and an idea occurred to her.

"I know Papa would enjoy these flowers," she thought. "I can't go to his room, but he hasn't forbidden me to speak to him. Perhaps I can find him in the parlor or the library, when he is by himself, and I can give him the blossoms before they fade."

Her opportunity came several hours later, after she had finished her school lessons. Passing the library door, she saw her father sitting there alone, reading. Though fearful that he might reject her gift, Elsie was determined to make her gesture of reconciliation, so she ran upstairs to her room, quickly plucked two perfect blossoms from her plant, and hastened back to the library. Her heart pounding, she crossed the soft carpet so quietly that her father did not hear her approach. When she reached his chair, he looked up with an expression of surprise.

"Dear Papa," Elsie began in a trembling voice, "the plant that Mr. Travilla gave me has bloomed at last, and I wanted you to have the first flowers. Will you accept them as a token of my affection, Papa?"

But before she had finished her words, Elsie could see the storm gathering in her father's face.

"No, Elsie," he said in a tone as cold as she had ever heard, "I cannot accept your flowers. They are a false token of love from a daughter who has shown herself ready to see

125

her father die rather than give up her willfulness. You know what I want from you, Elsie, and it is not flowers."

He turned his face away, and Elsie stood for a few moments, too stunned by the hardness of his words to move. Then her emotions burst from her. "But I do love you, Papa. You know I love you more than anything in the whole world!" she sobbed.

"Hush!" he commanded, drawing back in his chair. "And stop that crying. Miss Day tells me that you are ruining your eyes with your constant tears. If you don't stop, I will punish you severely. Besides, you have only your own misconduct to blame for your unhappiness. Take your flowers and leave me now. As soon as you are ready to submit unconditionally to my authority, you shall enjoy all my affection and care as before. But *not until then*, Elsie. Not until then."

Still clutching the flowers in her hand, Elsie had no choice but to do as she had been told.

Chloe was in Elsie's room, and when the child entered — her small face streaked with tears and two wilted, bruised blossoms dangling from her hand — the nursemaid immediately guessed something of what had happened. Opening her arms, she held the little girl and wiped at the tears with her handkerchief.

"Papa has told me . . . not to cry," Elsie said in little gasps, "but I . . . I can't help it, Aunt Chloe!"

"Jesus will help you," Chloe said gently. "He helps all His children to bear their troubles, and He never forsakes us. But you must try to obey Mr. Horace, child, because he is your father. You remember what your Bible says? It says, 'Children, obey your parents in everything, for this pleases the Lord.'"

"I know, Aunt Chloe, and I will try. But will you pray for me, Aunt Chloe, for it is very difficult."

And Elsie did work to obey her father's command. Even when she was alone, she struggled mightily to restrain her feelings and her tears. She was not always successful, but as she battled with her immense sorrow, she sought answers to her difficulties. She remembered these words from the book of Psalms: "God is our refuge and strength, an ever-present help in trouble." And she turned more and more to her Bible and her Heavenly Friend. Deprived of Horace's company, Elsie spent her time with God and His Word, and there she found "the peace that transcends all understanding." With the peace of God in her heart, her ability to meet the trials of each day was renewed and strengthened.

Horace had no such place of refuge and peace, yet his struggle was every bit as difficult as Elsie's. More difficult, in fact, because Horace had been cruelly misled by someone who had neither his interests nor his daughter's in her heart.

Mrs. Dinsmore could not be accused of slighting Horace's physical care. She was an excellent nurse, attending to all her patient's needs during his long illness. Indeed, Doctor Barton credited her in good measure for Horace's survival, and even Aunt Chloe had seen Mrs. Dinsmore push aside her own exhaustion to stay at Horace's side day and night throughout his fever and until his recovery was assured.

But Mrs. Dinsmore's good deeds only masked her jealous heart. She had always resented Horace, the stepson who caused so much trouble in his youth yet rated so highly in his father's esteem. When Horace had been sent away to college — after his early marriage and before the birth of his child — Mrs. Dinsmore had secretly welcomed his departure from Roselands. Then, just when she thought that Horace might never trouble her again, his daughter had appeared like an orphan on the doorstep, and all of Mrs. Dinsmore's bitter resentment had been turned upon the child.

Had the child been ugly, Mrs. Dinsmore might have shown more sympathy, for she always found pleasure in looking down on the less fortunate. But Elsie was a lovely child who would become a beautiful woman. It didn't help that Elsie was an heiress who would someday have wealth far beyond anything Mrs. Dinsmore's own daughters could hope for. Most important, Elsie was gifted with a gentle temperament and instinctive kindness that were foreign to Mrs. Dinsmore's understanding. With poisonous, little words — "so meek and spineless," "so lacking the Dinsmore strength of character," "such a rigid little Christian" — Mrs. Dinsmore had gradually succeeded in turning her husband against the child, and she encouraged her own children to taunt and tease the little intruder. Her own unfair and even abusive attitude was apparent to everyone except her husband.

Horace's return to Roselands had put an end to Mrs. Dinsmore's open campaign against Elsie, but the woman did not cease looking for opportunities to undermine the child's new position in her father's affections. (In fact, Horace had mistrusted Elsie at the start because, during his long absence from Roselands, Mrs. Dinsmore had frequently written to him with reports of Elsie's "misbehavior" and "false piety.") The conflict between Horace and Elsie, followed so closely by his near-fatal illness, had presented Mrs. Dinsmore with her chance.

While caring for Horace, Mrs. Dinsmore had carefully separated him from his daughter. When Horace, in his fevered delirium, had called for his little Elsie, Mrs. Dinsmore told him that the girl would not obey his commands or answer his wishes. She even forbade Adelaide to mention Elsie in his presence, and never told Horace of Elsie's pitiful pleas to see him.

Throughout his recovery, Mrs. Dinsmore continually conveyed stories about Elsie's haughty refusal to do Horace's bidding and seeming lack of concern about his health. False stories, but they were persuasive to an ill man who had not laid eyes on his child for weeks. On occasion, Horace would express doubts about his harsh punishment of Elsie, but his stepmother would assure him of the rightness of his actions. "Elsie is a willful and disobedient child," Mrs. Dinsmore would say. "If you don't use a firm hand now, she will grow up miserable and selfish." "You have to break her will," the woman would counsel, "before it breaks her." She even reminded him of his own stubborn nature and his dead wife's willful behavior in marrying him secretly, hinting that Elsie's obstinacy was natural to her character.

And so, like the serpent in the garden, she sowed doubt and distrust. Weak in body and soul, Horace felt his heart hardening. He loved Elsie — even Mrs. Dinsmore's false witness could not change that — but he became convinced that for her own good, he must win this terrible conflict. For Elsie's sake, he must rule her like a tyrant and refuse her all signs of his love until she bent to his will.

Elsie's Impossible Choice

Neither Elsie, nor anyone else, knew of Mrs. Dinsmore's influence. Only Adelaide, who had felt some vague doubts about her mother's motives, might have seen the truth. But soon after Horace had passed out of danger, Adelaide and Lora left Roselands to visit a family friend, and they would not return for several more weeks.

No one but the servants, who loved Elsie dearly, treated her with kindness and sympathy. Her grandfather ignored her entirely, and the other children, even Walter, constantly reminded her of her disobedience. She gave up her daily walks and rides with them until her father — told by Mrs. Dinsmore that Elsie was growing pale and unhealthy — reprimanded his child and commanded that she continue her daily exercises with the others.

Elsie obeyed without protest, but the change in her father was the most bitter of all her trials. And in time, her health did suffer. Love had made her bloom like her rare flower; now deprived of all signs of her father's affections, she withered. Her face grew thin; her cheeks lost their glow; and her eyes seemed clouded with sadness.

Through it all, Elsie often wondered if anyone could help her. Where, she asked herself, was Mr. Travilla? She hadn't seen him in a very long time, since before her father's crisis. The truth was that Edward Travilla had been called away to the North shortly after his last visit, and he knew nothing of the events at Roselands.

On his return home, Edward learned about Horace's serious illness and slow recovery, and he rode immediately to Roselands to see his good friend. He found Horace in the library, looking weak and depressed.

"Ah, my dear fellow, I came as soon as I heard you'd been ill, and I can see you are far from well yet," Edward exclaimed in his hearty manner. "Yet I am sure your little Elsie is the best of nurses. Where is she?"

"I no longer need nursing," Horace said shortly, then quickly changed the subject. The two old friends chatted for some time, and Edward was pleased to see the color rise in Horace's face and his eyes recover some of their normal animation.

After an hour or so, Edward looked at his watch. "I mustn't overstay my welcome," he said, "but I wonder if I might see my little friend before I go. I have a gift for her."

Instantly, the color drained from Horace's face, and his smile vanished as he replied, "I thank you, friend, but I prefer you not to give her anything now. Elsie has been very rebellious and stubborn of late, and she doesn't deserve your gift."

Edward was confused. "Can this be possible?" he asked. "I would not believe such behavior of her except that I hear it from her father."

"It's true," Horace said, sinking back into his easy chair with a long sigh. "Edward, I love that child as I have never loved anyone except her dear mother, and it cuts me to the quick to have her rebel as she has done for the last five weeks. I thought that she loved me too, but it seems I was wrong. She simply refuses to obey me, and surely obedience is the best test of love."

He paused for a few moments, then struggled to go on. "I have been forced to banish her from my presence. But, Edward, I can't banish her from my heart! I miss her every moment!"

Elsie's Impossible Choice

Edward was deeply concerned by his friend's obvious anguish. "I am truly sorry," he said, "but I have no doubt of her love for you. Let's hope that she will do her duty soon."

"Thank you. I can always count on your understanding in any kind of trouble," Horace said with a little smile that warmed his face for a moment. "But let's talk of something else."

Edward lingered a while longer, but he refused Horace's invitation to dinner, promising instead to return soon for a stay of several days. He was genuinely troubled by what he had heard from Horace. What could have happened between his little friend and her father? What new misunderstanding had caused this rift? One thing Edward did know — that he would pay his promised visit to Roselands as soon as possible. Perhaps he might be able to do something to resolve this painful problem.

A few days later, Elsie was walking down the hall on her way to the garden when she caught sight of her father sitting alone in the drawing room. She dared not make a sound, but she couldn't resist stopping in the doorway to gaze at the man whose companionship she missed so terribly. He sat very still, staring out the window, and in the sunlight, Elsie saw how drawn his face was, how pale in the strong light. He had the look of a man many years older and worn down with cares.

Elsie longed to rush to him, to beg his forgiveness, and promise to do everything he asked of her in the future. She might have given in to this impulse had not a hand grabbed her shoulder painfully and pulled her away.

"How dare you disturb your poor father?" Mrs. Dinsmore demanded in a low and hateful whisper.

"I wasn't disturbing him," Elsie protested, as she instinctively tried to shrug off the steely fingers. "I just saw him, and he looks so sad and ill and — "

"And if he does, it is all *your* doing, you miserable girl. Nothing ails him now but you and your perverse, obstinate selfishness."

Mrs. Dinsmore fairly spat out her words. She released her grasp, and Elsie instantly turned away and dashed down the hall and out of the house. Great, hot tears poured from her eyes as she ran through the garden to her favorite seat in the lilac arbor. So anguished was she that she didn't see Edward Travilla sitting on the bench there. She was almost upon him when she saw him, and she turned to run away, but he caught her dress and pulled her toward him.

"Don't run away, my little friend," Edward said in his kindly fashion. "Sit here beside me and tell me the cause of your tears. I may be able to help you."

Elsie, too tired now to resist, sat down, though she couldn't bring herself to look into Edward's face. He laid his arm around her trembling shoulders, and with his handkerchief, he began to wipe at her tears. His actions reminded her so much of her father's old gentleness that she burst into a fresh rain of tears.

"Poor child," Edward said, "calm yourself and then tell me what I can do for you. Won't you tell me the cause of this grief?"

As her sobbing subsided, Elsie was finally able to speak. "It's Papa, Mr. Travilla. He is so angry with me, and I've made him look so sad."

Elsie's Impossible Choice

"But what is the source of his displeasure, child? Surely if you have done wrong, you have only to confess and ask for his forgiveness. Then all will be right again."

When Elsie made no reply, he went on. "We all do wrong at some time, Elsie, and the noble way is to acknowledge our fault and ask for pardon. You know," he added more gravely, "that the Bible teaches us that children must obey their parents."

"Yes, sir. I know that the Bible tells me to obey my father," Elsie responded. "And I do try to obey him in everything that is right. But sometimes Papa commands me to do something that disobeys God, and the Bible says, 'We must obey God rather than men.'"

"So it does, Elsie," Edward agreed, "but have you considered that you may be too inclined to judge right and wrong for yourself? Life, as you will learn, is often complicated, and decisions between what is good and bad are not always as clear as you may think now. You are still a very young girl, Elsie, and your father is much older and wiser. I think it may be better to leave these matters to him until you are old enough to make your own decisions.

"Besides," he added thoughtfully, "If your father should bid you to do a wrong — and I'm not saying he has done so — then the responsibility would be *his*. He would have to account for it — not you."

Elsie thought about what Edward had said. "But Mr. Travilla," she finally replied, "doesn't the Bible teach us that each of us will give an account of himself to God? So I — not Papa or anyone else — will have to give account of my sins."

Edward stared into Elsie's eyes, no longer tear-filled, but dark and grave. He felt uncomfortable, for the child argued with reason and conviction far beyond her years. "I should know better than to try and quote Scripture to you," he said, lightening his tone, "for you are much more expert at that. But I am very anxious to see this conflict between you and your father resolved. You are both so dear to me, and I cannot bear your unhappiness.

"You have a good father," he continued, "and you can be proud of him. He is the most high-minded and honorable man I know, and I'm positive he would never require you to do anything he believed to be wrong. Won't you tell me exactly what has happened between the two of you?"

In truth, Elsie welcomed this opportunity to share her burden, for Edward Travilla had already proved to be a true and caring friend to her. So she told the story simply: "One Sabbath morning when he was ill — before he became so very ill — he asked me to read him a newspaper that was not fit for the Lord's Day. I couldn't do it, Mr. Travilla. I couldn't go against God's commandment to keep the Sabbath day holy. But Papa says I must apologize for not obeying him. And I must promise *never* to disobey him in the future. Until I promise, I am banished from his affection. But I can't do what Papa asks. No matter how much I love my Papa, I can't chose him over God."

There was no defiance in her voice. Edward heard only sorrow in Elsie's words and tone, so he knew that this was not a matter of childish willfulness.

"But if reading that newspaper to your father really were a sin," he said soothingly, "surely it would be a very little one. I can't believe that God would be angry with you for such a small thing."

"But, Mr. Travilla," Elsie replied, "if only you knew how much I *want* to obey Papa. But my conscience tells me it is wrong!"

Elsie's Impossible Choice

Edward hardly knew what to say, but as he tried to form a fresh argument, his thoughts were interrupted by the sound of steps on the gravel path. Elsie heard them, too, and the next moment her father entered the arbor.

Seeing his little girl sitting beside Edward sent a jealous chill to Horace's heart, and he was far more harsh than he intended when he demanded, "What are you doing here, Elsie? Crying again? Go to your room this instant, and stay there until you can show a cheerful face!"

Elsie obeyed without a word, or even a look at her father. When she had gone, Edward addressed his old friend: "Your daughter did not seek me out, Horace. She didn't even want to talk to me, but I detained her. Believe me, I have been trying my best to persuade her to submit to your commands."

"I doubt you succeeded," Horace said with a deep sigh. "I'm afraid that I shall be forced to use the most severe methods to break this obstinacy of hers."

"I'm sorry, Horace," Edward said, "but perhaps she has the right of it. She quoted Scripture until I had no more arguments to make."

Edward's response was not what Horace wanted to hear, and he replied fiercely, "I should think that the Fifth Commandment about honoring parents would be argument enough!"

"I don't say you are wrong, my friend," Edward answered in a conciliatory tone, "but we do not all see things the same way. I have to admit that in your place, I would do differently. Right or wrong, your child is acting from *principle* — not self-will. I think I would bend to her a bit in this circumstance."

"You think so? But you are wrong!" Horace exclaimed. "I can never give in to her. For her own sake, I must break her will, even though it breaks my own heart."

"And hers, too," Edward murmured to himself.

But Horace overheard the comment, and he responded with a hard little laugh, "There's no danger of breaking *her* heart, or she would have obeyed me long ago. But not even when I was so close to death, when I asked for her — not even then would she come to me."

Edward was astonished. "Are you sure she would not see you? You were so very ill. How can you know that?"

"I know," Horace replied, his voice harder than Edward had ever heard it. "Believe me, friend, I know."

Horace was so adamant that Edward realized it was useless to continue the conversation. Could Horace's statement really be true? Had Elsie refused to see her father in his time of need? Edward had come to Roselands hoping to mediate between father and child, but this war of wills appeared to be much worse than he had suspected. Much, much worse.

CHAPTER

9

Threats and Fears

"Jesus replied, 'If anyone loves me, he will obey my teaching."

JOHN 14:23

Threats and Fears

To Elsie and Horace Dinsmore, it seemed impossible that their situation could become much worse. They were locked in a stalemate, incapable of moving backward or forward because neither was able to relinquish the conviction of rightness.

Horace, in the depth of his heart, was determined that he must break Elsie's willfulness, or else he would be condemning her to a life of shallow and self-serving misery. Before him always was the vision of his own brother, Arthur, who had been raised without discipline, petted and pampered in every whim. And what had Arthur become? A weak and selfish boy, a gambler and a liar who lacked any shred of honor. No, Horace thought to himself whenever he was inclined to make peace with Elsie (which was more often than Elsie ever realized). No, he could not allow his own precious child to follow that pernicious path.

Elsie was every bit as unshakable as her father, convinced that Horace wanted her to chose between God and himself. As Edward Travilla had discovered, her knowledge of Scripture was extensive, and her faith was unwavering. Yet she was very young and still too inexperienced to know that God's Word required understanding of context, not just blind obedience. She had never before been faced with the possibility that her interpretation of God's commands might be faulty because it was incomplete. (She had read Jesus' statement that "it is lawful to do good on the Sabbath," for example, but it did not occur to her that reading a newspaper to her sick father might be doing "good.")

Elsie's Impossible Choice

Had father and daughter been able to talk together of their feelings and fears, they might have resolved their terrible dilemma. But Horace's harsh punishment allowed only the most basic of conversation, chiefly when he was chiding her for some small failing. As he maintained the distance between himself and his child — thinking that deprivation would compel her obedience — Elsie shrank away from him, finding her comfort and strength in her Bible and her prayers.

Though Horace, in his pride, tried to keep the whole matter to himself, it soon became obvious to even casual observers that something was amiss between the handsome young father and his beautiful child. One afternoon, Mrs. Dulcie Grey — an old acquaintance of the Dinsmores — called at Roselands. After Elsie had paid her respects to the good lady and departed from the drawing room, Mrs. Grey inquired of Horace, "Has your little Elsie been ill too, Mr. Dinsmore? She appears very thin, and she seems to have lost her bright color."

Horace was startled. "She has made no complaint," he said, "so I hardly think there is anything wrong with her."

"Perhaps not," Mrs. Grey replied thoughtfully, "but if she were my child, I should be afraid for her health."

"Whatever are you thinking, Dulcie?" said Mrs. Dinsmore with a mocking laugh. "Why, Elsie has always been a remarkably healthy child."

"Then I may be mistaken," Mrs. Grey said, rising to take her leave. Horace accompanied her to her carriage. Catching his eye as Horace helped her to her seat, the lady said pointedly, "I should be very sad if any illness were to come upon such a dear, sweet child as Elsie."

Mrs. Grey departed, but the force of her words lingered with Horace. Had Elsie changed, and he not even noticed?

Threats and Fears

Though loathe to share his concerns with others, he returned to the drawing room in a clear state of agitation. Mrs. Dinsmore, ever ready to drive the wedge between her stepson and Elsie deeper, said in the kindest of tones, "I see that Dulcie's remark has unsettled you, Horace. But Dulcie is always seeing trouble where none exists. Pay her no mind."

Horace crumpled into a chair and raised his hands to his temples. This new worry had set his head throbbing.

"But Mrs. Grey may be right," Horace said anxiously. "Elsie is thin and pale, I believe, though I have commanded her to take her exercise and I know she obeys. Oh, why did I ever start this dreadful business?"

"Because you are a good father," Mrs. Dinsmore replied. "Elsie must learn to submit to your will, and after all, you have done nothing to harm her. If she suffers, it is from her own obstinacy, and not your just punishment."

"But what am I to do with her?" Horace demanded, his voice cracking with emotion. "How can I correct this stubbornness of hers without breaking both our hearts?"

"You are too dramatic," Mrs. Dinsmore said, keeping her voice soft and full of sympathy. "There are other punishments you may use, for Elsie seems not yet convinced of your seriousness. A good spanking, perhaps."

Horace looked up quickly. "I would never lay a hand to her!" he exclaimed.

"Of course not," soothed Mrs. Dinsmore. "Then what of a boarding school? There are quite good schools where willful children learn to accept discipline and value the love of their parents. I believe that my Arthur will certainly benefit from his experience in boarding school and return to us a much more obedient boy." (In truth, Mrs. Dinsmore believed no such thing. Of all the reasons for her hatred of Elsie, Arthur's disgrace and banishment from Roselands was the most galling, and she blamed Elsie entirely for Arthur's troubles.)

"I have hinted at boarding school," Horace said, "and the idea does seem to frighten her. But it is my last resort, for I love her too well to give her into the care of strangers. You don't know how tempted I am to give this all up, to kiss her and forgive her and let it all be over and done. What other choice have I?"

Mrs. Dinsmore, fearful that Elsie might again have her own way, hastily assured Horace, "But you would not hurt her so, for it would be a hurt if you allow Elsie to triumph. You must stick to your course, Horace, however hard it is. For your daughter's sake. There is one measure you might take, although —"

"Tell me," Horace demanded. "I welcome any suggestion."

Mrs. Dinsmore began slowly, as if this new idea had only just come to her. "Well, I do think that Aunt Chloe is part of the problem. She is a wonderful nursemaid, of course, but she supports Elsie in this obstinate refusal to obey you. You must remember, Horace, that Chloe learned her principles from the same source as Elsie — that old-fashioned Scotswoman Mrs. Murray. I am sure that Chloe is encouraging the child now to think herself a martyr to principle. I have seen how Elsie runs to her nursemaid whenever you exercise your rightful parental authority and how Chloe lets her cry and sob. Perhaps if Elsie were entirely removed from Aunt Chloe's influence . . ." She let her words trail off.

For several minutes, Horace sat in silence, and Mrs. Dinsmore waited patiently for his reaction.

Threats and Fears

"I think there is wisdom in your thoughts," he said finally, "and I appreciate your suggestion. I owe Chloe a debt of gratitude for her excellent care of Elsie and her mother before her. I would hate to separate her from Elsie, but if all else fails, it may be necessary."

"Then let us hope that Elsie comes to her senses soon, before such an action is required," Mrs. Dinsmore said gently.

Except for her refusal to make the promise Horace wanted — the promise of complete, unconditional obedience to his commands — Elsie did everything in her power to be his dutiful daughter. Still, Horace found fault, punishing her for minor failings that would never have troubled him in the past, and looking, it seemed, for any excuse to exercise his authority.

One morning at breakfast, Elsie's grandfather drew a letter from the mailbag and was about to hand it to the little girl when Horace intervened. "From now on," he said coldly as he put the envelope into his coat pocket, "*I* am to receive all of Elsie's letters."

Elsie could only lower her head and struggle to finish her meal. Later, alone in her room, she gave vent to her feelings. Never before had she been so overcome with this angry desire to rebel against her father. She knew that the letter was from Rose Allison, for she had been waiting anxiously for words from her good friend. Now, when she so desperately needed Rose's love and sympathy, he had taken it from her. The disappointment was almost too great to endure.

Elsie was distracted all that morning. In the schoolroom, she recited poorly and received a stern rebuke from Miss

Day. But Elsie hardly noticed; her thoughts were on the letter and her father's unfairness.

By dinnertime, her anger had quieted, and she determined to see her father and politely ask for her letter. But Horace was not at the table that day, for he had gone into the city on business. When he returned in the afternoon, he was accompanied by several men. It was not until after supper that Elsie found her chance to approach Horace.

Her whole body trembling with fear, she went quietly to where he sat alone in the library, reading his newspaper. In words so soft they were almost inaudible, she said, "Papa, may I speak to you?"

Without looking at her, he replied, "Yes, Elsie, what do you want?"

"Please, Papa, may I have my letter now? I know it is from Miss Rose, and I have waited so long to hear from her."

Horace said nothing, and Elsie could not see the muscles in his jaw tighten. So she asked again, "May I have my letter, please?"

With a movement so sudden it made Elsie jump, Horace slammed his newspaper into his lap and turned to stare at her.

"Yes, Elsie, you may have your letter and everything else you want, the instant you show yourself ready to obey me. You have only to apologize for your refusal to obey me on that Sabbath day and promise your unconditional submission to my authority in the future. Do that, Elsie, and all will be restored to you. But there can be no *if's* or *but's* in your obedience."

Tears sprang into Elsie's eyes, but she resolutely fought them back. Once more she asked, "But may I not just read Miss Rose's letter? May I see it for just a few moments?"

"You have my answer, and it is all you will get."

Elsie knew better than to try again. She turned to go, but Horace called her back. His voice was quiet but cold as ice. "From now on," he said, "you are neither to send or receive any letters unless I see them first. And I cannot allow you to correspond with Miss Allison until you have become a more dutiful child."

"But what will Miss Rose think if I don't answer her?" Elsie exclaimed, her tears now flowing uncontrolled.

"I shall wait awhile to see if your behavior changes," Horace said. "But if it doesn't, then I shall write Miss Allison myself and explain the cause. I'm sure she will understand my reasons."

His threat horrified Elsie. "Please don't, Papa!" she pleaded.

"It is up to you, Elsie," he replied sternly. "Now go to your room. I do not want to see you again tonight."

Elsie was so distraught she could not speak, but only turned away. Suddenly an arm encircled her waist, and Horace drew her close to his side. In his old, loving tone, he said, "Dearest Daughter, why will you not give up this will-fulness and be my own sweet child once more? I love you so, and it hurts me more than you can imagine to see you so unhappy."

With his arm around her, Elsie let her head drop upon her father's shoulder. She stood very still, warm in the security of his love that had been absent from her life for such a long time. Never had she been so inclined to make the promise he wanted. With just a few words she could end her banishment. She would no longer face his punishments, no longer dread the possibility that she might be sent away from him forever. With just a few words, she would be

147

enclosed once more in the circle of his love and approval. It would be so easy to restore her father's precious love. But what of the love of Jesus? What of His love which was the most precious of all?

The temptation was great, but it passed quickly, and she spoke in a voice choked with emotion. "There is no one in the world I could ever love as much as I love you, Papa. And I want always to be your obedient daughter. But Jesus tells us that the first and greatest command is to love Him. He says, 'Anyone who loves his father or mother more than me is not worthy of me.' I must love Jesus best and keep His commandments always. Oh, Papa, I can't say I'm sorry that I didn't break His commandment. If you loved Jesus, Papa, you would understand me. I can't choose to obey you and not Him. Please don't ask me to make that choice."

Horace had dropped his arm before she finished, and now he sat stiffly erect in his chair. He was so angry that he could not look into her face. "You are a child, Elsie, and the Bible commands you to obey *me*, your father and guardian. Yet you persist in this belief that *you* know what is best. Well, if love and affection will not change you, then you force me to take more severe measures. You shall learn that I am a man of my word, whatever the cost."

At that he rose and quickly stalked out of the room. Elsie could only stare dumbly at the door. When the sound of his footsteps had died away, she ran to her own room, but there was little comfort for her this night. Not Aunt Chloe's gentle embrace. Not even the words of her fervent prayers could drive the awful fear from Elsie's heart.

Aunt Chloe had often reassured Elsie that this trial was part of God's plan and that God would see her through it. But Elsie could not imagine any plan that brought so much suffering. Her faith was strong, but still she raised her questions to God. "What have I done to deserve my Papa's anger?" she asked. "Am I wrong to refuse to obey him? Am I wrong about Your commandments? How can I go on without my Papa's love?"

Horace's fury and his promise of more severe punishment terrified her. More than anything he might do, she feared separation and felt that she would surely die if she could not be near her Papa. She could bear his anger and his coldness so long as she could at least see his face and hope that someday his heart would be changed. But what would happen if he sent her away from him? Who else would give her shelter?

It was then that she remembered a verse from Proverbs, and the words calmed her fears and renewed her hope: "The name of the Lord is a strong tower; the righteous run to it and are safe." She imagined a tower of strength that offered refuge from all her earthly trials. Then she reminded herself that Jesus had felt the pain of separation from His Father when He bore the sins of mankind on the Cross. Whatever happened, Elsie knew that Jesus would not forsake her. With these thoughts, she slipped into a peaceful sleep.

Horace Dinsmore found no such rest. After Elsie's most recent defiance, he had retreated to his room where he paced the floor late into the night. Finally falling upon his bed, he closed his eyes, but the image of his child and the memory of her words haunted him like an unforgiving ghost. He had given her every chance to repent of her obstinacy, and still she refused. The time had come to act on his threats, though he hated the mere thought of causing his dear child more pain. But it had to be done . . . had to be done . . . for her sake —

At length he slept, but it was not the peaceful sleep that Elsie had won. Horace tossed and turned; his dreams were vivid reflections of his anger and sorrow and fear. He woke with dawn's light, more tired than when he had gone to bed, yet determined that he would pass not even one more day awaiting Elsie's promise of obedience. He would act, and he would act now.

CHAPTER

10

A Sudden Departure

"In my distress I called to the Lord; I cried to my God for help."

PSALM 18:6

A Sudden Departure

*F*or some time, little seemed to change in Elsie's routine. Her father's business took him away from Roselands more often than usual, but since she no longer enjoyed his companionship, Elsie was barely aware of these absences. In truth, however, changes were taking place that would soon alter everything.

It happened that Mr. Granville, the owner of a large estate located not far from Roselands, was planning to move his family to another part of the country. Mr. Granville was most anxious to sell his plantation, and he had approached Horace as a possible buyer. The two men had quickly come to an arrangement that was mutually satisfactory, and as soon as the sale was complete, Horace began making improvements to his new property.

Horace had inherited money from his late mother, so he was able to spend lavishly on these improvements. In addition to the usual repairs to farm and fields, Horace undertook an extensive renovation of the large estate house, adding all the modern conveniences and furnishing the mansion in the most elegant style.

As news of his purchase of The Oaks — for that was the name of the plantation — circulated in the neighborhood, a rumor quickly spread that he was preparing to bring home a new wife. Some people even speculated that this was the cause of Elsie's altered appearance, her pale face and sad expression. Horace, of course, had no such intention.

"I need a housekeeper," he said to Mrs. Dinsmore one afternoon as they sat together in the drawing room. "And I've decided to send Aunt Chloe to The Oaks. She will do very well to manage the house, and this will give me the opportunity to separate her from Elsie for the time being."

Mrs. Dinsmore could barely contain her satisfaction at Horace's announcement. "I hope *you* do not plan to leave us soon," she said, careful to hide any note of falseness in her voice.

"Not for a while," he replied. "I must end this conflict with Elsie first, and I believe the prospect of a new home with me will help convince her to change her position."

For all the confidence he expressed to his stepmother, Horace inwardly shrank from the knowledge of how his action would affect Elsie. He knew that separation from Chloe would cause his daughter terrible grief. Yet he was absolutely persuaded of the rightness of his course, and the very next morning, he summoned Chloe to his room.

When he had informed her of his purchase of The Oaks, Horace explained that he planned to send her there as housekeeper in charge of the estate house and the servants. Chloe was both surprised and highly flattered by this proof of Horace's confidence. She immediately expressed her thanks and her readiness to undertake her new responsibilities. Then a thought stuck her, and she asked, "Will Miss Elsie be going with me?"

"No!" Horace declared, more forcefully than he intended.

Shyly but with conviction, Chloe said, "Then, sir, I think I ought to stay here, for there's no one else to care for my little child."

"I'm sorry, Chloe, but you really have no choice in the matter," Horace stated. "You must pack your things and be prepared to leave after dinner today. I have instructed Jim to drive you there in the carriage."

Chloe couldn't stop herself, but blurted out in trembling words, "But why, sir? What have I done to displease you so? What is the reason for you to part me from the child I've loved since the day she was born?"

Horace was deeply moved by the nursemaid's distress. He remained decided as ever, but responded to her with genuine kindness, "You've done nothing wrong, Chloe. Indeed, I owe you greatly for the care you have given both to my child and to my dear wife. Believe me, I have no intention of hurting you, but I judge that a separation from Elsie is best for her at present. I do not do this lightly, and I am hoping that it won't be a lengthy separation. But as much as I regret the pain this is causing you, it must be done."

Chloe could hear in his voice that nothing would change his mind. Protest was useless, so with a simple, "Yes, sir," she left to prepare for her departure.

An hour later, when the morning's school lessons ended, Elsie returned to her room and was surprised to find Chloe hurriedly packing a trunk.

"What is it, Aunt Chloe?" she asked. "Are we going somewhere?"

Chloe did not raise her head, but continued to fold a starched white apron, as she said softly, "Not us, darling. *I'm* going away for awhile. Your father is sending me to his new place to be housekeeper, so we are going to be apart for a while."

Elsie was stunned. She could barely conceive of life without her beloved Aunt Chloe. There had never been a day when they were not together. Not even an hour when she could not count on her faithful nursemaid to be close at hand.

"But why?" Elsie cried. "You can't go! You can't! Nobody loves me but you, Aunt Chloe. You can't leave me!"

Chloe's heart nearly broke at these words. She moved to take Elsie in her arms and hug her close. "I don't know why, precious, but perhaps it won't be for very long."

Elsie would not be comforted. "I must talk to Papa," she sobbed. "I'll beg him to let you stay!"

"It's no use doing that, child. His mind is settled, and I'm leaving today. Now, don't you go making new trouble for yourself."

But Elsie broke from her arms and ran into the hall, determined to confront her father and demand that Chloe stay. In the corridor, however, she found a servant who informed her that Horace had already gone and would not return to Roselands till suppertime. So there was nothing to do but return to her room and spend these last few hours with her dearest friend.

Chloe, who had always provided solace and wisdom when Elsie was troubled, could find no words of comfort this time. Her grief was every bit as deep as Elsie's. She was wracked as well by anger at Horace and by a growing fear that this separation would never be repaired. (Chloe was a slave, and long before she had been given charge of Elsie, she had experienced the bitter despair of being taken from her family to serve others. Sitting now, rocking Elsie in her lap and weeping her own hot tears, Chloe felt the pain doubly because her memory took her back to another time and other grievous partings from those she loved.)

At last there came a tap on the door and Jim entered to say that Chloe's carriage was waiting. The young man lifted

Chloe's heavy trunk and left quickly, before the girl and the woman could see the tears in his own eyes. Elsie only gripped Chloe tighter, as if to anchor her nursemaid to the spot.

"Don't do that now, child," Chloe pleaded. "You're going to break my heart!" She took Elsie's wet face in both her strong hands, and looked into the little girl's eyes. "Now it's time for me to go. We must ask the Lord to bring us together again soon, Elsie darling. We must pray very hard, and I'm sure He will answer our prayers before long."

Her voice dropping into a husky whisper, Chloe said, "We must trust in the Lord now, and put all our faith in Him." Then she gently disengaged herself from Elsie's grasp and walked from the room.

Elsie was left alone. Alone as she had never before been in her life.

Fanny, a young servant who had always felt a special affection for Elsie, had been assigned by Horace to take Aunt Chloe's place and provide for his child. Fanny knew that no one could take Chloe's place in Elsie's heart, but she determined to do her best. She helped Elsie dress for her ride that afternoon and was there to greet the little girl after her exercise. She saw to it that a good supper was brought to Elsie's room that evening, and she coaxed her new charge to eat. But Elsie was more like a broken doll than a human child. She could barely move, for her arms and legs felt as heavy as lead. Her head ached from crying and grief, and the mere thought of food made her stomach rebel. She was hardly aware when Fanny dressed her in a clean, white nightgown and brushed back her curls. She hardly noticed when Fanny tucked her into bed and kissed her lightly on the forehead. She hardly heard when Fanny said, "You go on to sleep now, Miss Elsie. I'll be back later to turn out the lamps."

But Elsie couldn't sleep. She was overwhelmed with her desolation. She longed for the warm arms, the generous smile, and the loving heart that had been her rock since infancy. She yearned to lay her aching head on Chloe's broad shoulder and pour out all her sorrows.

Unable to rest, she got out of her bed and went to the floor-length window that opened onto the balcony. Perhaps some fresh air would relieve this throbbing in her head. She stepped outside, and the cool night air did seem to help a little. Leaning against the high balcony railing, she murmured to herself, "Oh, Aunt Chloe, why did you leave me? How can I live without you, without anyone to love me?"

A low voice answered, "Elsie, I know you think me a cruel father to send your Aunt Chloe away." Horace walked close to her side.

"I know you have the right to do as you will, Papa," Elsie said, "and I'll do my best to submit to your decision. But I can't help feeling very sad, Papa."

"I understand, Daughter, and I take no pleasure in causing you sorrow. But I have good reasons for my action. You have resisted my authority for so long now, that I want you to have new influences. I fear that Chloe, while intending no harm, has tacitly encouraged your rebellion. So for your sake, I must keep you two apart until you have learned obedience."

Elsie was astonished at this explanation. "But, Papa, Aunt Chloe would never support me in disobeying you.

She's always taught me to yield a ready and cheerful obedience to *all* your commands and wishes, unless they are contrary to God's Word."

Horace stiffened. "There!" he said sternly. "That is just it. Aunt Chloe and that Mrs. Murray brought you up to believe that you and they are wiser than your own father. That you and they are more capable of interpreting the Bible and judging right from wrong. But *they* are wrong, Elsie, and you must accept *my* authority."

Fearful of giving way to his frustration, Horace turned to go, but Elsie ran to him, clutching his hand and begging, "Please stay, Papa. I am so alone. Please stay, Papa, and give me just one little kiss!"

Horace could not stop himself. He reached down and lifted Elsie into his arms. He cradled her head on his shoulder and carried her back to her bed. Without speaking, he tucked the blankets about her and kissed her warm cheek. Then he turned and left, shutting the door behind him.

Far from comforting, Horace's brief tenderness only made Elsie's loneliness more acute. Reminded of his love, she felt her losses like new knives to her heart, and her body was convulsed with sobbing. Her head pounded, but just when she thought the pain might kill her, a voice more gentle than the softest spring breeze whispered, "Never will I leave you; never will I forsake you." She listened, and the voice came again, "When your father and mother forsake you, the Lord will receive you." At these words, Elsie's sobs subsided, and her head began to clear. Then the voice spoke once more: "As a mother comforts her child, so will I comfort you."

And Elsie fell asleep.

CHAPTER

11

All Hope
Lost

*"'For I know the plans I have for
you,' declares the Lord, 'plans
to prosper you and not to
harm you, plans to give
you hope and a
future.'"*

JEREMIAH 29:11

orace, a young man who had so much of earthly treasures, lacked the greatest treasure of all. Unlike his daughter, he had no Heavenly Comforter to call on in his suffering, no personal knowledge of the One who hears all prayers and brings peace and consolation. Horace had only himself for counsel, and after his brief meeting with Elsie, he went to his room alone and confused.

Truly, this conflict with Elsie was breaking his heart, and he was not at all certain that he could resist her much longer. Why, he could barely even remember the cause of their quarrel. Yet to give in now, he told himself, would be to condemn his child to a lifetime of willful and manipulative selfishness. The image of Miss Stevens, the Christmas guest, came into his mind. Lovely and gifted the lady was, but totally self-centered and bent upon having her own way without any thoughts of others. No! Elsie must not be allowed to become like Miss Stevens. Willfulness in the child would become intolerable conceit in the adult. It was his responsibility, Horace told himself firmly, and his deepest obligation to his dead wife, to see that Elsie grew into a caring and dutiful woman. He simply could not compromise his principles when Elsie's lifelong happiness was at stake.

As he paced the room, arguing point upon point in his own mind, Horace's glance fell upon some papers on his desk. They were letters from his agents in the North asking for instructions about matters relating to Horace's new estate. There was also a note from an old college friend requesting Horace to pay a visit on his next trip to that part of the country. Horace had intended to handle his business affairs by writing, but now as he looked at the letters, he saw a solution. He would journey northward immediately and meet personally with his agents. He would accept his old friend's invitation to visit. Most important, he would separate himself from Elsie. It would be hard for him to leave her for long, but his absence would surely break her will and secure her obedience. She would realize how important her father's love and companionship were, and once she submitted to him, all would be well again.

Horace dared not give himself time to contemplate his decision, knowing that his desire to be with his child might shake his resolve. He consulted the sailing schedule that he kept in his desk, then summoned John and gave the servant his orders.

"Pack light clothes, for we will likely be gone well into the heat of summer. We will leave for the city tomorrow," Horace informed the surprised man, "and I believe we can still book passage on the ship that departs the day after."

Then Horace went to find his father, to tell the old gentleman of his journey. Horace decided not to explain the true motive for the trip. There was no need to burden his father or the rest of the family with his private troubles.

Elsie was served breakfast in her room the next morning, so she knew nothing of Horace's plans until, on her way to the schoolroom, she encountered John carrying her father's trunk and several boxes.

"John!" she exclaimed. "Is Papa going away?"

"Yes, Miss Elsie," John replied happily, for he always looked forward to the excitement of travel. "Aren't you going along, too?"

Elsie couldn't speak. First Chloe, now her father. She felt as if she had been hit in the stomach, and for a moment, she feared that she might become ill. "Where . . . where is he going?" she finally managed to stammer.

"Up North, Miss Elsie," John said kindly. He had seen her face go ashen and understood instantly that the news had come as a shock. "I'm sorry I don't know more about it. You best go ask your daddy."

Horace emerged from his doorway at that moment, and Elsie rushed to him, tears streaming down her face. "Oh, Papa!" she cried. "Are you going away? Are you leaving me?"

Horace took her hand and gently guided her back into his room, closing the door. He led her to his chair, and taking his seat, lifted her onto his knee. His face was almost as pale as hers, but he wore a look of firm determination.

"I must go, Elsie," he said. "I have important business to attend to up North. And I also believe that time apart from me will cure you of your rebellion."

"But how long will you be gone?" she begged.

"That is entirely up to you. Should you apologize and promise to obey me this minute, I will gladly take you with me. But I cannot take a willful child on my travels. So I ask once more. Will you promise me your unconditional obedience?"

"In everything, Papa, except —"

He cut her off. "Hush! If you will not submit now, then you must contemplate your duty on your own. When you have changed your mind, all you need do is write me a letter,

and I shall start for home that very day. But not until I hear from you."

He set her on the floor and moved to the door. "I will say good-bye to you now, and wait for your answer. Your grandfather has the address at which I can be reached."

Elsie cried out to him, "Then kiss me good-bye, Papa! Please! Just one kiss!"

Without turning to look back at her, he said coldly, "It would be a wasted kiss, Elsie, from one who does not love her father well enough to obey his commands." And quickly, he left. But he was never to forget her pitiful cry; it would haunt him for the rest of his life.

Elsie slumped into her father's chair and made no effort to control her tears. It was not long before the sound of the carriage wheels on the drive reached her ears. She listened until the sound vanished, and in the stillness of Horace's room, all she could hear was the pounding of her own heart. The thing she feared most had happened: her father had left her. As terrible as the last months had been, she had at least had the comfort of knowing that her father was nearby, that she could see his face across the table and hear his steps in the hall. She had been afraid he would send her away to boarding school, but this was worse. *He* had left — left her here where no one loved her or cared whether she lived or died. She would die, she thought, without his presence. She would die and go to Heaven and be with God and her mother forever.

The tears she shed on the day of her father's leaving seemed to be her last. In the days that followed, she was always dry-eyed, as if she had emptied the well of sorrow. She rarely spoke to anyone, and except for Fanny, no one sought out her company. Even Adelaide and Lora, who returned from their visit on the day after Horace's departure, kept their distance. (Not from lack of affection, however. Both young women had been convinced that it was Horace's wish for Elsie to be left to herself — the better to see the error of her ways.) But Adelaide noticed the decline in her niece. The dull eyes and thinness were plain enough, but more troubling was Elsie's new apathy. The child seemed to have lost interest in life itself and moved about the house like a wispy shadow.

"I wish Elsie would perk up," Mrs. Dinsmore said one day as she and Adelaide watched the little girl walk into the garden. "Horace really should have sent her off to boarding school. Since he left, she sulks around here and depresses everyone. What a constant irritation she is."

"I'm becoming very concerned about her," Adelaide replied with feeling. "She's losing too much weight. Just yesterday I found Fanny in Elsie's room, and she was crying. She was altering a dress of Elsie's, and she was crying as she showed me how much she had to take in the dress so it would fit. She said that Elsie barely eats anything and is so weak that the least exercise exhausts her. I really think we should write to Horace."

"Nonsense, my dear!" Mrs. Dinsmore huffed. "Children always seem to grow thin and languid in weather as hot as this, and I suppose fretting about her father has taken Elsie's appetite. Besides, with school ended for the summer, she has nothing to occupy her time. She is merely bored, Adelaide. Horace spoiled her dreadfully last summer, remember. Now trust me. She'll soon get over this lethargy, so there is no reason at all to trouble Horace. Believe me, Adelaide, I have many years' experience with children, and there's nothing wrong with Elsie."

Assured that her mother must know best in these matters, Adelaide decided to delay writing to Horace. But she did not entirely stop watching her little niece.

Adelaide was not the only one to notice the changes in Elsie. A few days later, Edward Travilla returned home to Ion several hours later than expected. When he entered the parlor to greet his mother, that good woman sensed immediately that something disturbed him. His step lacked it usual quickness, and his tone when he addressed her did not convey its usual liveliness. When he sat down beside her, she saw that his face was troubled and he seemed to be entirely distracted.

Laying her hand on his, she inquired, "Are you well, my son?"

"*I* am perfectly fine," he replied with a sad smile. "It is the well being of another that concerns me."

"Who?" Mrs. Travilla asked.

"I have just come from Roselands, where I saw our little friend Elsie. I had but a few moments with her, just long enough to say hello. Mother, that child is so changed that you would hardly recognize her. She has grown very pale and thin, and the worst of it is that she seems to have lost all her gaiety and animation. When I spoke to her, it was as if she did not even understand my words. She smiled at me, but with such a dreary and hopeless smile."

"What has caused this change?" Mrs. Travilla asked, herself now as concerned as her son, for she had a deep affection for little Elsie and knew from Edward of the little girl's recent troubles. "What is Horace doing for her?"

"That's just the problem, Mother. Horace left a week or so ago for the North, and no one has any idea when he will return. His trip seems to be some kind of punishment for Elsie, but I declare the child is utterly shattered by his absence."

Then Edward had an idea. "Mother, you must go to her. She trusts you, and she needs just the kind of help and advice you can give. Will you go?"

"Gladly, Edward. I will go this moment if you think necessary."

"Best wait till tomorrow," he said. "I learned from Pompey that the whole family, except Elsie, will be going into the city then, and frankly, I think it would be much easier for Elsie if you talk to her alone. I doubt that even Mrs. Dinsmore would forbid you to see the child, but I fear she might make a private conversation impossible. It seems that Horace left orders that his daughter is not to receive guests nor go visiting until he comes home."

Edward turned his deep gaze on his mother. "Horace is my closest friend," he said seriously, "and I know him perhaps better than anyone. But I cannot imagine what he hopes to accomplish with this dreadful separation. He will truly break her heart before he breaks her will."

Late the next morning, the Travillas' carriage pulled up at Roselands. Pompey came to greet the guests, and he was clearly surprised to see them.

"Mr. and Mrs. Dinsmore and the children are not at home," he said apologetically, though he was sure he had conveyed this information to Mr. Travilla only the day before. "Just Miss Elsie is here, but if you'd like to come into the drawing room, I will get you some mighty good refreshments."

Edward said, "My mother has come to see Miss Elsie."

"She's up in her room right now, ma'am," Pompey said to Mrs. Travilla. "I'll have Fanny summon her."

Mrs. Travilla replied, "No, Pompey, I will go up to her room, and you see to my son. I think he might enjoy a glass of your cool lemonade."

The lady then disappeared into the house and quickly found her way upstairs. The door to Elsie's room was open, but Mrs. Travilla stopped short when she saw the child. Elsie was sitting in her rosewood rocking chair. Her head lay back, and she seemed to be staring at nothing. An open book rested on the floor where it had fallen from her hand.

Edward's description had not prepared Mrs. Travilla for what she beheld. The child appeared to have lost half her weight since Christmas, and her face was so thin that the cheekbones seemed ready to break through. And the eyes — those once bright, hazel eyes — were dark and dull as if a veil had been drawn across them.

Quietly, Mrs. Travilla entered. Taking Elsie's hand, she led the child to the couch where they could sit side by side. Instinctively, Mrs. Travilla drew Elsie close, into a warm and motherly embrace. As she kissed the little girl's forehead, a hot tear fell from her own eye onto Elsie's cheek.

Elsie looked up. "Don't cry, Mrs. Travilla. I *never* cry anymore."

"And why not, darling? Tears are often a blessed relief to an aching heart, and I think it would do you good to cry. Those dry eyes need it."

"Oh, no, ma'am. I can't. My tears have all dried up, and that's good because they always displeased my Papa."

170

There was such hopelessness in Elsie's voice, and when she smiled, Mrs. Travilla saw the dreariness and sorrow of which Edward had spoken. Anxious to restore hope to her little friend, the elderly lady hugged Elsie closer and said, "You must not give way to despair, my dear. Your troubles have not come by chance. The Lord who loves you has allowed them. Remember His promises, Elsie; God will never abandon you in your time of need."

"Do you think He could be angry with me?" Elsie asked fearfully. "Could God be unhappy with me for loving my Papa too well?"

"No, dearest. God would never be angry with you for loving your father. Although we cannot see the reason for your trial now, someday we will understand it. When we go home to our Father's house, everything will be made plain. It may be, Elsie, that by your steady adherence to what you believe is right, you will be the instrument to bring your father to a saving knowledge of Christ. God moves in mysterious ways, my child — ways that we cannot expect to understand in this life."

"But I'm afraid that I'll never see Papa again. Never!" With those desperate words, Elsie groaned, and her whole body convulsed with sobbing.

Mrs. Travilla was greatly relieved by this flood of tears, for she knew that crying was far better than the child's unnatural apathy. She held and soothed Elsie for some time, and when the sobs had finally quieted, she said, "You will see your father again, dear girl. I am sure of that. God is the hearer of prayers, and He will hear your prayers to be reunited with your father. You must put your trust in your Heavenly Father, Elsie."

"Do you think Papa will come back to me soon?" Elsie asked in a hopeful tone.

"I cannot say when, dear child. It is all in God's hands, and He will do what is best for you and your father. I cannot say when your suffering will end, but everything God allows, He allows out of His love for you."

Mrs. Travilla's words were like a balm, and when Elsie begged the good woman to stay a bit longer, Mrs. Travilla was glad to comply. "I will come again soon, and perhaps you could visit us at Ion. You could spend the rest of your holidays with us, for both Edward and I would be delighted to have your company. Shall I speak to your grandfather?"

"That would be wonderful," Elsie said quietly, "but it's impossible. My Papa said that I can't have guests or go visiting until he comes back."

"Oh, dear," Mrs. Travilla said in embarrassment. "Edward mentioned that, but I quite forgot. Then I cannot even visit you again. But I will ask Edward to write to your father, and perhaps Horace will give permission for you to come to Ion."

In a tone of resignation, Elsie responded, "I don't think he will. My Papa never breaks his word or changes his mind."

Mrs. Travilla was afraid that Elsie was correct; Horace could be hard as stone when he was convinced of his own rightness. But she said, "If you cannot come to us, you must remember that you are always in our hearts. And Elsie, you always have the loving presence of our precious Savior. With Him beside you, no one can make you wholly miserable."

With that, she hugged Elsie close once more and kissed her tenderly. "I must go now," Mrs. Travilla said at last, "but God will bless and keep you always, darling Elsie, and we shall both pray to see each other again very soon."

In the carriage on the road back to Ion, Edward turned anxiously to his mother. "Well, what do you think?"

"I found her in just the state you described," Mrs. Travilla affirmed. "She is deeply depressed, though I think I helped her a bit. She seemed less wretched when I left. But what does Horace Dinsmore think he is doing?" she said with a flare of anger. "What does he hope to achieve by devastating his own child?

"I think you should write to him immediately," she went on. "If he will not come home, at least he might permit Elsie to stay with us at Ion for a few weeks. Will you write him?"

Edward was thoughtful. "If you think it best, I will," he said, "but I worry that it may do more harm than good. Horace is stubborn, as you know, and jealous of any interference, especially between himself and his child. I fear that such a request from me will only make him more determined to have his way. It may make the situation worse for Elsie."

His mother sighed. "You're right," she conceded. "It will take something more powerful than you or I to change his mind. But we can pray for Elsie. We must pray for her."

⌒

Mrs. Travilla's visit had been like a reviving tonic for Elsie. It roused her from despair and gave her a new light of hope. Her father's departure had come so suddenly that it had nearly crushed her spirit, but Mrs. Travilla reminded her of the precious promises and tender love that were still hers — the love of her Heavenly Father who would never allow her to suffer without cause and would end her pain as soon as His plan was accomplished.

Elsie's Impossible Choice

Elsie went to her Bible and found these words: "For it has been granted to you on behalf of Christ not only to believe on Him, but also to suffer for Him." It was clear to her now that she was suffering for His sake, that her trials had come because she loved Him and would not betray His commands even to please her dear Papa. Her endurance was an act of love, and endure she must, for she could not betray her Savior even though loving Him was not always easy. In God's Word, she found the promise that "the God of all grace, who called you to His eternal glory in Christ, after you have suffered a little while, will Himself restore you." She cried again, but for the first time in a very long while, her tears came from thankfulness, because she had again found a promise in God's Word to sustain her.

Elsie's situation at Roselands was not altered by Mrs. Travilla's visit, for Pompey kept that information to himself. (After all, the servant reasoned, it was not Elsie's fault that guests had arrived when the family was away, and Elsie had done only what was polite in receiving Mrs. Travilla.) But for many days afterward, Elsie seemed a bit more like her old self. Fanny was pleased to see that the child was eating a little more, though she was still painfully thin. Each day, Lora tried to seek Elsie out for an hour of Bible reading, and Adelaide was always kind when she encountered her little niece. On several occasions, Adelaide joined Elsie and Lora for their Bible study, and the young woman appeared most thoughtful at the words she heard.

The rest of the family ignored Elsie as usual. Mr. and Mrs. Dinsmore spoke to her only to scold, and apart from Lora, the children deliberately excluded her from their games and activities. So Elsie was mostly alone. Mrs. Travilla had brought her such comfort, but as the days dragged by, Elsie was more and more consumed with thoughts of her absent Papa. It was summer once again, but how different from the last summer when she and her Papa had traveled and he had shown her so many new and interesting places and things. He had loved her then. Would he ever love her again? Would he ever return so she could see his face and hear his voice? Would this separation never end?

The temptation to write to her father and submit to his will grew stronger. Only a few words, and he would come back to her. Her terrible trial would be ended. She had to wage a fierce battle with herself each time the easy solution tempted her. She prayed fervently for the strength to resist, but gradually her agonizing struggle wore her down.

One morning after breakfast, Mrs. Dinsmore came to Elsie's room. Curtly dismissing Fanny, the woman waited until the door was closed, then drew an envelope from her pocket. Elsie saw instantly that the handwriting on the thick package was her father's.

"Horace has asked me to deliver this to you," Mrs. Dinsmore said, holding the envelope out for Elsie to take. "Read it, and when you are finished, prepare yourself for a carriage ride. I will follow your father's instructions to the letter, so I expect you downstairs and ready to depart at eleven o'clock sharp. Do you understand, girl?"

"Yes, ma'am," Elsie said shyly, and without another word, Mrs. Dinsmore swept from the room.

Elsie's hands were trembling as she gazed at her name, written in strong, black script on the creamy white envelope. She was desperate to read her father's words, yet terrified of what they might say. Without Mrs. Dinsmore's command, Elsie might have delayed opening the letter until she was more calm. But she had to be ready in an hour — for what she could not guess — and so she carefully unsealed the envelope and drew out the sheets.

Horace's letter was kind, even affectionate, but it brought no comfort. Horace wrote at length about The Oaks and the improvements he was making to the estate. He was having a suite prepared and furnished for her, and he expressed his hope that they might live there together. He planned, he said, to become her teacher himself, so there would be no need for a governess. And, of course, Aunt Chloe would again have special charge of Elsie. He painted a beautiful picture of his new home and the happy life they could share at The Oaks.

Then he wrote that his determination to correct her willfulness was unaltered. If Elsie still refused to submit entirely to his authority, he would be forced to move alone to The Oaks, and she would be sent to a boarding school, far from family and friends. The choice, he said, was hers alone.

To help with her decision, however, he had asked Mrs. Dinsmore to take her to The Oaks so that she might see the beauty of his new home. Elsie was to judge for herself the type of life she could enjoy there — loved and taught by him — and only then to decide. His final instruction was that she should have as long as a month to consider. If he had not heard from her after that time, he would assume that her choice was made.

Elsie was torn. Her father's words promised a virtual paradise on earth. But the alternative! To be sent away into the care of strangers who could not be expected to love her or be sympathetic to her faith. (She was convinced that her father, in his determination to root out her beliefs, would select a boarding school where God was a stranger.) It was too terrible to consider. But if she chose what her heart longed for — to be restored to her father's affection — she must betray her higher duty and pledge to accept her father's commands over God's. Did ever a child face such a dreadful decision?

Quickly she found her Bible and turned to the Book of Isaiah. There! There were the words she remembered: "I, even I, am He who comforts you. Who are you that you fear mortal men, the sons of men, who are but grass, that you forget the Lord your Maker, who stretched out the heavens and laid the foundations of the earth."

She could not forget her Maker; she could never abandon the One who loved and sustained her every hour and minute and second of her life. "I need not fear the consequences of following the commands of the Lord," she said to herself with fresh determination. "But help me to be strong, Lord Jesus. Please help me to be strong."

She closed the little book, and with her strength renewed, she left her room and went to meet Mrs. Dinsmore.

A short time later, the Roselands carriage turned into a long drive shaded on both sides by tall oak trees that seemed to bend their long branches overhead like sheltering arms. After some moments, the trees suddenly opened onto a beautiful setting in the midst of which was a large and handsome house of dark gray stone. The carriage came to a halt in the columned portico at the front of the house. As Ajax, the driver, helped first Mrs. Dinsmore, then Elsie to the ground, Elsie saw that the mansion sat on a rise, and dipping away on all sides were brilliant green fields. In the fresh air, she caught a faint scent of the sea.

"Oh, how lovely," she whispered to herself.

Elsie's Impossible Choice

At that moment, the door opened, and Aunt Chloe came forward, beaming with happiness at seeing Elsie after so many weeks. But Chloe was careful not to offend Mrs. Dinsmore and addressed the older woman. "It is good to welcome you to Mr. Horace's home, ma'am," she said graciously. "He wrote that you'd be coming by with Miss Elsie. I suppose you would like some tea before you tour the place."

Mrs. Dinsmore, scowling with impatience, brushed past Chloe and mounted the steps. "No tour for me, thank you. I have been in this house many times in the past. I shall have tea in the parlor, Chloe, while you show the place to Elsie. And do be quick about it. I am much too busy to waste time on a silly mission such as this, and I do it only as a favor to Horace."

Chloe and Elsie, following in Mrs. Dinsmore's wake, exchanged knowing smiles. When Chloe had settled the lady comfortably in the parlor and ordered her tea, she took Elsie's hand, and they left, closing the parlor doors tightly behind them. Wordlessly but with great exuberance and many hugs and kisses, the nursemaid and her charge were reunited. Picking Elsie up, Chloe carried her into another room, and an expression of concern replaced the bright smile on her face.

"Child, you're as light as a feather," Chloe said as she put Elsie down. "And your face is looking mighty peaked. You been eating like you should? Is Fanny taking care of you?"

"I'm just fine, Aunt Chloe, especially now," Elsie replied. "And Fanny is very kind to me. Kinder than almost anyone now that you have gone from Roselands."

Chloe was not satisfied, for she could see the pale color and stress in the child's face. But she checked herself and made no further comment about Elsie's appearance.

Instead, she began to describe the beauties of The Oaks, starting where they were in Horace's study. As they progressed from room to room — drawing room, library, second parlor, sitting rooms and bedrooms — Elsie was astonished at the luxury of the place. No convenience had been overlooked, and every nook and cranny was decorated in the best of taste. Chloe took her to the kitchen and pantry and on to the servants' rooms. They toured the grounds — the vegetable and flower gardens, the hothouse, and the grape arbor. Then they returned to the rooms that were to belong to Elsie: bedroom, sitting room, and dressing room, all furnished just as Elsie would have wanted.

As they stood in the large bedroom, Elsie gazed on the elegant four-poster bed which was draped in satin and lace covers, the handsome carved chests and night tables, the large couch covered in elegant silk brocade. It was a room fit for a princess, and Horace had spared no expense to make it perfect in every detail.

"I've missed you so, little girl," Chloe said, at last daring to mention their painful separation. "But now the good Lord has brought you back to me, and you'll be as happy here as ever a child could be."

Tears sprung into Elsie's eyes. "But I won't be staying," she said.

"You'll be coming back soon, though?" Chloe questioned. "I'm sure Mr. Horace plans to return now that the work on the house is finished, and I know he wants you here."

"No, Aunt Chloe. Papa says that I must give up my willfulness and obey his every command. If I don't, I'll be sent away to boarding school, and this will never be my home." With these words, Elsie threw herself into Chloe's arms and cried bitterly.

Elsie's Impossible Choice

The nursemaid was too astonished to offer her usual words of comfort. "But how can that be?" she demanded of no one. "I thought for sure your troubles were over. I thought your Papa must have seen the rightness of your thinking and made his peace with you. Why else would he have made this beautiful place for you?"

They clutched one another in silence for several minutes until Chloe, wiping the tears from Elsie's cheeks, said, "We must be moving along now. I've got one more place to show you, and Mrs. Dinsmore will be getting all itchy if we don't get back soon."

The last rooms were her father's suite, and again, everything was done to perfection. Elsie could almost see her father in the sitting room, surrounded by his books and paintings. There was a piano in the corner, and Chloe begged her to play a little tune. It had been so long since the nursemaid had heard her child's sweet music.

Chloe could not stop her own tears as Elsie played and sang a song that was one of the nursemaid's favorites, a Scottish air that both had heard first from Mrs. Murray. When the song was done, Chloe led Elsie to another side of the room where a drape had been pulled over the wall. Carefully, Chloe drew the cloth back and revealed a life-sized portrait of Horace Dinsmore. So close was the painting to the look of the man that Elsie jumped back. "Papa!" she cried. "Oh, Papa! Can you know how much I miss you?"

Chloe bent down and hugged the girl as Elsie sobbed, "It's so hard, Aunt Chloe, to know I may never see him again. Never live in this beautiful house with him!"

"My poor, poor child," Chloe said. "I do believe that it will all come right by-and-by. And you got to believe it, too.

180

You got to trust in the Lord. He can change your father's heart and incline him to respect your principles. I know He can, and you got to believe He will."

Elsie sobbed out her fear of boarding school — so lonely and so full of worldly temptations. But Chloe reminded her of the Lord's words: "Be strong and courageous. Do not be terrified; do not be discouraged, for the Lord your God will be with you wherever you go."

"Think now, Elsie child," Chloe said. "If He is with you, who can hurt you? Just nobody!"

"You're right, Aunt Chloe," Elsie said, feeling a little better. "The Lord is my refuge, and I shall try very hard not to be afraid."

They hugged again and then began to walk back to the parlor. As they passed a tall window, Elsie stopped and tugged at Chloe's hand. She pointed out to the yard where a giant oak tree stood, its spreading foliage shading a broad patch of the lawn.

"Do you see that tree?" Elsie asked. When Chloe nodded, Elsie continued. "I want to be buried right there, in the cool shade, where Papa can see me every day and remember me always."

"What are you talking about?" Chloe exclaimed in astonishment. "You're too young to be thinking of things like that."

"My Mamma was young when she died," Elsie said in a dreamy voice. "I know it's not right, but sometimes I think how nice it would be to lie down and be with Mamma and Jesus forever. They would love me always. And I'd never be lonely again."

Chloe had become truly frightened at Elsie's words, but she struggled to make her voice light and cheerful. "Now you just put those ideas away right now," she said. "You put your trust in the Lord, and He will make things right and bring you back to me soon. We're going to be happy again, I just know."

Elsie, her eyes dry now, looked into her nursemaid's face and smiled. "Thank you, Aunt Chloe," she whispered, "for loving me so. I have to be going now. Mrs. Dinsmore is waiting."

There was nothing for Chloe to do but bid her beloved child farewell. As the Roselands carriage disappeared down the drive, the nursemaid found herself shivering, although the heat of the day was at its peak. "Something is very wrong," she said to herself sorrowfully, "and I don't know how to put it right. It's up to you, Lord, to save that poor child now."

CHAPTER

12

Desperate Days

*"My comfort in my suffering
is this: Your promise
preserves my life."*

PSALM 119:50

During the return trip from The Oaks, there was no talk between Elsie and Mrs. Dinsmore. For her part, Mrs. Dinsmore was far too put out by the venture to waste her words on its cause. And Elsie had slipped too deep into her private despair for polite conversation. On reaching Roselands, Elsie went directly to her room and her Bible. But this time she sought not comfort and hope, but release.

She turned to the Book of Matthew and the record of Jesus in the garden of Gethsemane. "My soul is overwhelmed with sorrow to the point of death," she read, and her own tears fell in grief for the pain of her beloved Savior. In her own way, she understood the bitterness of His cry, "My Father, if it is possible, may this cup be taken from me." She wept at His submission; "My Father, if it is not possible for this cup to be taken away unless I drink it, may your will be done."

Elsie read the passage again and again. Could she bear her own suffering with the same perfect submission as her Beloved Lord? Would she endure her own final trial with the same patient spirit? She prayed with a fervor that left her drained and weak, and eventually she collapsed upon her bed. But she could not sleep nor even rest. She tossed and turned. Her head throbbed at visions that came and went in a fevered fury. The Oaks, her father's portrait, dark and distant rooms where God was banned and little girls were schooled in worldly philosophies. Her mind was filled with terrible sights, each dream worse than the last.

Just before suppertime, Fanny came in to dress her little mistress and found Elsie in a dreadful state. The child's cheeks burned, and her eyes glistened with fever. Badly frightened, Fanny rushed away in search of Adelaide, the only member of the family whom Fanny trusted to care about Elsie. Finding Adelaide alone in the library, Fanny burst out, "Please come, Miss Adelaide! Miss Elsie is bad sick, and I think she needs the doctor!"

Following the maid to Elsie's room, Adelaide immediately realized that the child was indeed seriously ill. Stroking Elsie's damp forehead with her cool hand, Adelaide whispered to Fanny, "Go quickly and find Jim. Tell him to ride for Doctor Barton immediately. And on his way back, he must stop at The Oaks and summon Aunt Chloe. Tell her to come as soon as she can."

Adelaide then set about making Elsie as comfortable as possible until Chloe and the doctor arrived. It was not more than an hour before Chloe entered the room and took over the nursing. Doctor Barton appeared soon after, and while he made his examination, Adelaide excused herself and went to find her parents.

Mr. and Mrs. Dinsmore were in the sitting room, and Mrs. Dinsmore was about to chastise Adelaide for missing supper. But Adelaide spoke first, "Elsie has taken a fever, and I summoned Aunt Chloe and Doctor Barton, who is with her now."

"A fever?" Mrs. Dinsmore exclaimed. "Is it contagious? Are my children in danger?"

"I don't know, Mamma, except that she appears very ill."

"Well, it is good that we are all packed for our holiday at the shore. I certainly don't want the others exposed to her illness, whatever it is. You know how dangerous these summer fevers are. We shall all leave first thing tomorrow morning. Can you be ready to leave after breakfast, my dear?"

"No, Mamma," Adelaide replied. "I will stay here with Elsie."

"But that's absurd! Aunt Chloe will care for her, so there's no reason for you to be exposed to any infection."

"I don't believe there's any danger, and Aunt Chloe will need my assistance," Adelaide said, her tone quiet but firm. "I will not leave Horace's child alone. Elsie means a great deal to me, and I cannot forsake her now."

"Then you should stay," spoke up Mr. Dinsmore. "I doubt that Elsie is contagious. Clearly the child has worried herself sick over her father's absence. Besides," he turned to his wife, "how would it look to the neighbors if we all run off and desert her when she is ill?"

This argument carried great weight with Mrs. Dinsmore, for she was always concerned about the opinion of others. However little she cared for Elsie, she did not want to be seen as thoughtless of her stepson's daughter.

At that moment, Doctor Barton entered the room, his face grave.

"Good evening," he said in greeting; then he turned to Mr. Dinsmore. "I think Elsie is quite sick, sir, but I cannot give you a precise diagnosis of her condition."

"Is it contagious?" Mrs. Dinsmore demanded.

"I can't say with certainty, madam, but I think not."

"Should we send for Horace?" Mr. Dinsmore asked.

"Not now," Doctor Barton replied. "This may be only a brief attack. Let's wait and see how she progresses."

Adelaide said nothing, but she had already resolved to write to Horace that very night.

Mrs. Dinsmore bid the doctor a hasty good-bye and left to complete preparations for the family's vacation. After a few more words with Mr. Dinsmore and Adelaide, Doctor

Barton promised to return in the early morning, then bade them farewell.

That night, Adelaide and Chloe took turns nursing Elsie. As the little girl tossed and turned and talked to herself in comments so garbled as to be incoherent, the two women applied cool compresses and soothing words and administered the medicine Doctor Barton had left. Just before dawn, as Chloe napped on her old cot, Adelaide sat beside Elsie's bed and prayed as she never had before.

Adelaide did not claim to be a dedicated Christian, but in recent weeks, as she sat with Elsie and Lora during their Bible study, she had found herself drawn to the sweet assurances of God's Holy Word. When she was alone, she read her own Bible with new attention and an increasingly open heart. In God's Word, she sensed a cleansing and loving spirit that was greater, more satisfying than any of the material pleasures she had always enjoyed. Now, in this crisis, she poured out her heart to "the Father of Compassion," begging that He might spare this lovely child and open Horace's eyes to the rightness of Elsie's cause. Asking nothing for herself, she prayed in true Christian spirit that Elsie's life be saved, and if that was not to be, that Elsie would spend eternity in her loving Heavenly Father's embrace.

When the day broke, Elsie at last fell into a calm sleep. Adelaide looked into the wan but peaceful little face on the pillow and prayed that this was the beginning of her niece's recovery. Adelaide was determined to stay by Elsie's side until the little girl was fully back to good health, but she had little confidence in her own nursing skills. Adelaide always helped her mother whenever the other children were sick and had assisted through Horace's illness, but she had never carried the full weight upon her young shoulders. The rest of the family would be leaving in just a couple of hours, and whom could she turn to then for advice and wisdom?

Elsie slept for some time, and Chloe, fresh from her rest, took over the watching and waiting while Adelaide went downstairs to see the family off. Everyone was in high spirits, excited by the prospect of a holiday at the seaside, and except for Lora, no one seemed at all concerned about Elsie. When they had gone, Adelaide breakfasted, though she had no appetite, and while she was at the table, Doctor Barton arrived, and with him a most welcome guest.

"The doctor stopped by Ion on his way here," said Mrs. Travilla, "and told us of Elsie's illness. I prevailed on him to bring me along. I hope I may be of some help to you, dear."

Adelaide rose and rushed into the woman's open arms. "Oh, I am so glad you are here, Mrs. Travilla," she declared. "I had been praying for someone wiser than I, and here you are — the answer to my prayers!"

The two women conversed quietly while the doctor went to see his patient.

"But Horace must be notified immediately," Mrs. Travilla said on hearing what had occurred since she last saw Elsie.

"I wrote him last night, and Pompey has already posted my letter, and I shall write to him every day until he returns," Adelaide said forcefully. "I just know that he is the medicine Elsie really needs, and surely he will come home when he knows how ill she is."

"I confess I find it hard to understand his position," Mrs. Travilla replied, "for Elsie has never defied him except for moral principle. He is a moral man, and he should appreciate her strong principles."

"Perhaps he remembers his own willful youth," Adelaide said softly.

"Well, we shall pray that he receives your letter soon and makes an immediate return," Mrs. Travilla answered. "Till then, we must devote all our attention to Elsie and her recovery. And you, dear Adelaide, must take care of yourself. I want you to get some rest now, for I can see you had a sleepless night. Trust me, I will summon you should anything change."

Sadly, things did change. Elsie's fever returned, in spite of Doctor Barton's medications, and as the fever raged, she drifted in and out of delirium. She didn't recognize anyone and seemed to be haunted by dreadful dreams. Once she sat straight up in bed, and grabbing Mrs. Travilla's arm, she screamed, "Don't do it, Papa! Please don't send me away!" Then she collapsed back into fevered tossing.

It was some days before the fever subsided and Doctor Barton judged her to be out of danger for the moment. Confidently he prescribed rest and a nutritious diet to restore her health. In truth, a great many tears of joy were shed that day. But no matter what the doctor and the women did, Elsie did not recover. The fever was down, but her strength continued to decline until at times she seemed too weak to open her eyes. She never cried and rarely spoke, and the only pleasure she seemed to find was in having her favorite Bible passages read to her. Repeatedly she requested the story of Jesus' night in the garden of Gethsemane, and each time these words were read — "may your will be done" — her face took on a strange expression of calm.

Doctor Barton shook his head. He, Adelaide, and Mrs. Travilla were together in the parlor.

"I must admit that I am deeply worried," he said. "There is no sign of improvement, and I have no medicines to supply what she needs. Why, that child seems to have lost her very will to live. She is just wasting away. There is a great sorrow pressing on her and sapping her life. Have you written to Horace?"

"I've written him every day since she became ill," Adelaide said. "I've sent letters to every address he left with Father — to his agents in New York and his friend in Baltimore. And still, there is no reply."

"I fear the worst if he does not come soon," the doctor said with immense sadness. "I have seen this happen in older people, when they give up the will to live."

"She is dying of a broken heart," Mrs. Travilla said almost in a whisper.

"That cannot happen!" Adelaide exclaimed. "We can't let that happen!" Without excusing herself, she ran from the room directly to the library. Taking paper and pen from the desk drawer, she wrote in a shaking hand: "Dear Brother, You *must* come home now if you hope to see your Elsie alive again. She seems to believe that this terrible illness will be her last, and I am afraid nothing can save her but your presence. You *must* save your child, Horace, and come the minute you receive this letter."

She quickly addressed the envelope in care of Horace's old friend in Baltimore, and then she called for Jim. He must ride to the city immediately and dispatch the letter by the first train.

Once Adelaide had calmed her nerves and repaired her face, for she was crying all the while she was writing her urgent appeal to Horace, she went to Elsie's room to relieve Fanny, who was taking a turn at the nursing.

At her aunt's entry, Elsie raised her head, and for a moment, Adelaide thought the child might be better. Her eyes certainly seemed brighter and clearer, and she wore a little smile.

"Aunt Adelaide, I'm so glad you've come," the child said in a hoarse whisper. "There is something I want you to do for me. Something I need to write. I'd do it myself, but I don't seem to have the strength. Will you help me?"

"With anything you ask," Adelaide said gently. "Shall I use your little writing desk?"

"Yes, please."

Adelaide quickly assembled all the materials she needed and took her seat close beside Elsie. "Now," the young aunt said in a cheerful tone. "Tell me what you want me to write."

An hour later, when Chloe came upstairs, she found Adelaide standing in the hall, a stack of papers and a little package gripped tightly in one hand. Adelaide's face was ashen and huge tears rolled down her cheeks.

"What is it?" Chloe cried out. "Is it my Elsie?"

"She is still with us, Aunt Chloe," Adelaide gasped. "But I fear it will not be for much longer. She has just told me that Horace will never return, that he will never forgive her. She is entirely without hope of seeing him again, and I could say nothing to comfort her."

Adelaide grabbed Chloe's hand in her own and held it to her cheek. "Go to her Aunt Chloe, and restore her hope if you can," Adelaide pleaded. "We can't give up on her! She can't leave us!"

Too overcome to say more, Adelaide retreated to her own room where she carefully folded the thick sheets of paper, tied them with a blue satin ribbon, and placed them with the package in the drawer of her bedside table. Then she sat on her bed and wept bitterly. Her tears were tears of fatigue and anguish and fear — mostly of fear, for Adelaide could not imagine life without the little girl whom she had come to love with her whole heart.

Late the next day, Elsie's fever returned, and she again became delirious. Doctor Barton was sent for, and the women did their best for her until the physician arrived. He stayed with Elsie for some time, and when he emerged from her room, Adelaide and Mrs. Travilla anxiously asked for his report.

"Her fever is high, and she has little strength to fight off this new infection," he began, "but I am not ready to give up yet. The medicines, I believe, will quell the fever. There is no immediate danger, but if I may impose upon you, I would like to stay with her tonight."

"Of course," Adelaide replied with great relief. "I'll have Fanny prepare Horace's room for you. It is just a few doors away."

"Thank you," said the kind man. "And now I have a prescription for you two ladies. Aunt Chloe and I will tend to Elsie tonight, so I want you both to have a good supper and get a full night's sleep. This illness, I fear, will not run its course for some time, and I need you to be strong for Elsie's sake."

Elsie's Impossible Choice

With several more reassurances that Elsie was not in immediate danger, he sent the two women off to eat and to rest. It was not necessary to ask for their prayers: they were all with Elsie that night.

CHAPTER

13

In the Hands of God

"The Lord is close to the brokenhearted and saves those who are crushed in spirit."

PSALM 34:18

*A*nd where was Horace all this time? Why had he not responded to Adelaide's impassioned pleas for his return?

It was not lack of love that kept Horace away. Rather, while visiting with his agents in New York, he had learned of an excellent business opportunity in Ohio and traveled to that state without notifying anyone of where he would be staying. And so Adelaide's letters had accumulated at the home of his friend in Baltimore, not to be opened by Horace until he arrived there on the day before Elsie's final relapse. But as soon as Horace arrived at his friend's, he was given the letters. Immediately he had read one or two, and in alarm, he called for his carriage. With a quick apology to his friend, Horace left for the train station to board the first train south.

His fellow passengers could not help but wonder at the obvious distress of the handsome young man. Constantly, he looked at his fine pocket watch, and each time the train stopped on its journey, he paced the aisle as if his own animation might spur the train onward.

Had the strangers on the train been capable of reading his mind, they would have seen the turmoil of a man in agony. "What have I caused?" he asked himself. "How could I have been so deluded by my pride? I am a *monster* to have so misunderstood my dear child. Only a *tyrant* could have demanded obedience in violation of her principles."

He read the remainder of Adelaide's letters — all but the last she wrote, which had not yet arrived at his friend's address — and berated himself for being so thoughtless and self-centered as to fail all this time to communicate with Roselands. The letters revealed how long Elsie had been ill, since the day he commanded that she visit The Oaks. What was he thinking to imagine that the mere promise of luxury would tempt her to give up her deepest beliefs?

The train moved swiftly through city and countryside, but not swiftly enough for Horace. He looked out the window and saw nothing save his daughter's beautiful face. "She is so young, so healthy," he thought. "It cannot be true that she is near death! No, it can't be! God would not send me so terrible an affliction!"

Early on the morning after Elsie's relapse, a carriage drove wildly up the drive of Roselands and halted at the door in a cloud of dust. Instinctively, Horace looked for the little girl who had always before waited for him on the steps and greeted him with such smiles of joy. But she was not there, and looking upward, he saw that the curtains at her bedroom window were drawn closed. Bounding up the portico steps, he mocked himself: "Of course she's not waiting for you. She is still ill. But I'm coming, Elsie, and you shall have all the love a father can give."

When Pompey opened the door, Horace barely gave the worried servant a glance, but raced up the stairway and to his daughter's room. Outside her door, he heard a laugh, *her* laugh, and for a moment his heart lifted. "She is better," he murmured to himself, "and now that I am here, she will soon be well." He put his hand to the knob and entered the room.

What a sight he beheld! Doctor Barton, Adelaide, Mrs. Travilla, and Chloe were clustered around the bed, holding down the hysterical child who struggled wildly under their caring hands. Elsie was laughing — an eerie, unnatural laugh that alternated with strange ravings and outcries. Could this be the child he had left? She was as thin and pale as a wraith; her eyes, sunk into her head, were ringed with shadows the color of bruises, and they flashed with fever.

None of the adults noticed his entrance, but as he approached the bed, Elsie caught sight of his face. Instantly she grabbed Adelaide's skirt and clung to her aunt as if seeking shelter from some terrifying creature. "He's come to take me away!" the little girl screamed. "Help me! Please save me from him!"

Quickly the doctor took Horace by the arm to lead him away. But Horace resisted. "Elsie! It is I!" he exclaimed. "It's your father come back to you!"

Elsie only grasped her aunt more tightly and turned her face away from him. He could see her frail body quaking, like a small animal cowering before a mad beast.

Stunned, Horace no longer resisted the physician's direction and was led away into the hall.

"What you see is the delirium of fever," the doctor said. "If she lives, it will go, and she will recover her reason."

"If she lives? Is there no hope?" Horace asked, his voice cracking with emotion.

"Do you want the truth?" Doctor Barton queried.

"Of course! I must know everything."

"Then I will be completely frank, Horace. Had you returned a week ago or even two days ago, before the return of the fever, there might have been some chance of saving her. But now, I fear for the worst. I have never seen anyone recover who was so ill."

Elsie's Impossible Choice

His face contorted with pain, Horace demanded, "But you must save her. Save her, and you shall have everything I am worth!"

Doctor Barton drew back and replied sharply, "You cannot *buy* her health back, Horace — not for all you possess. And you cannot command it. I am doing everything I know to do, but God alone can save her now. We must look to Him."

Horace fell into a chair and hung his head. In a voice soft with sorrow and regret, he said, "I'm sorry, Doctor. But if she dies, I will go to my grave guilty of murdering my own daughter with my cruelty. How could I have been so blind? How could I have insisted on obedience when it collided with her conscience? I thought I was right, but I was so terribly wrong."

"But there is life yet," the good doctor said with compassion. "Though human skill can do no more, He who raised the dead daughter of a synagogue ruler and restored the dead son of the widow of Nain — He can give your child back to you. I beg you to turn to Him, my friend. Turn to Jesus.

"Now I have to return to my patient. For the time being, I must ask you not to see her, for your presence seems to distress her considerably." Then the doctor added with gentle assurance, "Don't let that concern you. It is very common in cases like this for the patient to turn away from the very person she loves best. If there is a change in her condition, I will call for you instantly."

Horace could only retire to his room and await news of the fate of his beloved child. He had not eaten or changed his clothing for almost two days. Yet when John, who had accompanied his master on the journey from the North, brought a dinner tray, Horace turned it away. The distraught father had no stomach for food nor any concern for his personal comfort.

For hours he paced his room, his mind consumed with grief and self-reproach. At length, Adelaide entered, carrying a fresh tray of food. She was at first inclined to chastise her brother for his long delay in returning to Roselands, but his wretchedness softened her. When he asked her to stay for a few minutes, she gladly complied.

Horace explained to his sister why he had not answered her urgent letters, but he did not excuse himself. Then he asked for all the details of Elsie's illness and what had been done for her. Adelaide told him everything and dwelled especially on Elsie's longing for her Papa's return. As she spoke, Horace's dismay increased, and he rose from his chair to pace the room. Ever so often, a deep groan of anguish escaped his heaving chest.

Adelaide finished her recital, and for some time, the two were buried in silence. "I can never thank you enough, dearest sister," Horace said finally, "for the great kindness and care you have given my child."

"But, Horace, it is I who owe her the debt," Adelaide replied with intensity. "Elsie has given me the greatest gift of all, for she has brought me to the love of God! You know that I always loved her in my fashion. But since this terrible conflict began, she has taught me by her every word and deed what it is to be a true Christian. She has shown me the way to Heaven, and now she is going there before me. I am a better person for knowing her, and now I may lose her. Oh, Brother, I can't bear to lose her! I can't!"

Elsie's Impossible Choice

At this, Adelaide broke into tears, and Horace exclaimed, "Then you must hate and despise me for my cruel treatment of her!"

Calming herself, Adelaide gently laid her hand on her brother's trembling arm. "I could never hate you," she said tenderly. "I know that you never intended for this to happen, that you love Elsie with all your being. I am very sorry for you, dear Brother."

There was a light tap at the door, and Doctor Barton entered. "Horace," he said, "Elsie is calling for you, so come now. I think it possible that she may recognize you."

Eagerly Horace followed the doctor, and in seconds he knelt at his child's side.

The little girl's eyes were closed, and she was moving restlessly. She moaned, "Papa, will you never come back to me?"

"I'm here, darling," Horace said tenderly. "I have come back to you, and I will never leave you again."

She turned to look at him. "I want my Papa."

"I am here, dearest. Your Papa is here. Don't you know me?"

His voice was full of sweet emotion, but at his words, Elsie's eyes widened in terror, and she grabbed for Mrs. Travilla. "Make him go away!" she shrieked. "He's here to hurt me! He wants me to turn away from Jesus!"

"It's no use," Doctor Barton said sadly as he took Horace's arm and urged him away from the bedside. "She doesn't know you, and perhaps she never will."

That night and the next day, Horace was barred from Elsie's room. In his solitude, Horace paced his room, berating himself over and over for his heartlessness. He had never experienced agony such as this before, and for the first time he saw himself as God must — a wretched sinner, lost and ruined.

Horace's mother had been a pious woman, and her early influence had saved him from many of the temptations to which young people are exposed. He was in almost every respect a moral and honorable man, but he took intense pride in his morality and his scrupulous behavior. In his arrogance, he assumed that he deserved all the blessings of this world and would likely be blessed in the next. On those rare occasions when he tried to pray, it was always in the attitude of the Pharisee in the Book of Luke: "God, I thank you that I am not like other men." But now he saw where his pride and self-satisfaction had taken him.

He thought of his child — her deep humility, her stead-fast desire to do right, her genuine love of Jesus, her determination always to do her duty out of devotion to the Lord. Elsie was willing to part with everything she loved and esteemed rather than commit what to others might seem a very small sin. He contrasted her pure faith to his own self-righteousness, his neglect of the Savior, and his tyrannical determination to make Elsie as worldly proud as himself. Horace looked into his own soul, and what he saw there wrenched from him a cry of the deepest despair:

"God, be merciful to me, a sinner!"

It was the first *real* prayer he had ever offered.

Horace's terrible wait continued throughout the day. When she could, Adelaide came to him with reports of

Elsie's condition, and she encouraged him to dress and eat, for Elsie's sake. She brought him a dinner tray, and on it she had placed a little book — Elsie's Bible.

"I thought it might help to comfort you," she said.

At first, Horace could not trust himself even to look at the book that had always been his daughter's companion. He held it close to his chest, as if the book itself might yield up some of his child's warmth and love. At length, he opened it, and his heart throbbed. On its pages, he saw the many marks of her pencil, underlining the passages that meant so much to her, and the stains of her tears where she had wept in sorrow and joy.

He began to read, and as the hours passed, he was increasingly aware of the importance of the teachings and their application to his needs. Not that the words were comforting. In Ephesians, he read: "Fathers, do not exasperate your children; instead, bring them up in the training and instruction of the Lord." Horace looked back over his life and his treatment of Elsie, and he trembled. But he continued to study and learn. He had read these words all his life; he was an educated man who had always regarded the Bible as an interesting historical document. But now, for the first time, the truth of God's Word leapt at him from the worn pages of his child's little book. His eyes caught these words: "whenever anyone turns to the Lord, the veil is taken away." And Horace knew in the depths of his heart that he had lived his whole life to this moment shrouded in a veil of disbelief.

In a voice hoarse with emotion and tears, he prayed, "Forgive me, Lord Jesus. Take away my sins and spare my precious child!"

About midnight, Adelaide came to his room and found him dozing in his chair, the little Bible still clutched in his hand. Gently, she shook him awake.

"Elsie's fever has gone, and she has fallen asleep," Adelaide said.

Horace started up, a look of expectation brightening his face.

"It is not over yet, Brother," Adelaide cautioned. "Doctor Barton says that this is the crisis. There is a little hope that she may wake refreshed. But the Doctor fears that this may be the precursor of death."

"I must be with her," Horace exclaimed. "She won't know that I am in the room, but I must look on her dear face."

"No," Adelaide said firmly. "If she wakes and sees you — who knows that her excitement may not prove fatal? You must stay here, and I will come for you the minute she wakes."

Adelaide drew a bundle of papers and a package from beneath her apron and held them out to Horace. "Elsie entrusted these to me to be given to you on her death," she said, and tears began to roll from her eyes. "I believe you should have them now."

Horace took the items and looked questioningly at his sister.

"It is her last will and testament," Adelaide said, choking back her tears. "I wrote it for her when she was too weak to lift a pen. And there is a letter that she wrote on the afternoon she returned from seeing The Oaks. Whatever happens now, I believe you must have them."

Wiping her eyes, Adelaide left, and Horace stood staring at the bundles in his hand. He opened the package first and what he saw tore at his heart. It was his wife's miniature, the precious portrait that Elsie had worn around her neck every day that he had known her. And with it a lock of Elsie's own hair — a shining ringlet tied with a pure white, satin ribbon.

Pressing the ringlet to his lips, Horace sat down and opened the letter. There, in her familiar childish hand, he read:

> *Dear, dear, Papa,*
>
> *My heart is very sad tonight. How often I wish that you could look into my heart and see how full it is of love for you. I am always thinking of you and longing to be with you. I have done what you commanded and visited The Oaks today. I know how happy I would be there, or anywhere, with you, if you would only let me make God's law the rule of my life. I know how much your anger hurts me. How much more terrible would be the grief of my Heavenly Father if I betrayed His commands. I hope that you will not send me away to be among strangers. Although I cannot make the promise you require, I do promise to be good and to obey you in everything that my conscience allows. But I cannot choose your love over God's.*
>
> *If I am never to see you again, I want to ask your forgiveness for every naughty thought I ever had about you. Twice, I rebelled in my heart toward you — when you took away Miss Allison's letter and when you sent Aunt Chloe away. Although I was only angry for a little while, it was wrong of me and I am very, very sorry. Please forgive me and I will never indulge in such rebellious and angry feelings again.*

Horace slammed his free hand on the hard arm of his chair. "*She* asks my forgiveness," he said to himself in disbelief, "when it was *I* who so cruelly and thoughtlessly abused my authority. Oh, my poor child, that I may have the time to beg your forgiveness."

206

In the Hands of God

There was more in the letter, and after a few minutes, Horace read on:

If I should die, Papa, and never see you again in this world, please don't be angry with yourself. I know you have been severe with me because you want me to be good. And everything you have done has truly brought me closer to Jesus. When I am sad and lonely, He is always there for me. If I should die, and you feel sad and lonely, will you go to Jesus, too? He loves you and always will. And I will always love you, even if I never see you again.

Your daughter, Elsie

Never did a man repent so bitterly of harsh words and deeds. Horace covered his face with his hands as if to hold back his tears. But shame and regret overwhelmed him, and he wept like a child. Remorse ate into his very soul, and he would have gladly given his own life just to take back every cruel word and hard punishment he had ever imposed on his good and true child. In an instant, he would eagerly have given his life to save his Elsie.

CHAPTER

14

A New Beginning

"Praise be to the God and Father of our Lord Jesus Christ! In His great mercy He has given us new birth into a living hope through the resurrection of Jesus Christ from the dead, and into an inheritance that can never perish, spoil or fade."

1 PETER 1:3

A New Beginning

*H*orace was so deep in his painful thoughts that he did not hear the rustling noises and hushed voices that began to fill the house. From the entrance hall, a deep sigh and an old servant's whispered "Hallelujah"; from the drawing room, a quickly spoken prayer of thanks; from the kitchen pantry, a joyful shout of "Praise the Lord!"

In every room and corridor of Roselands, the word was being passed. Little Elsie was alive!

Without stopping to knock, Doctor Barton burst into Horace's room. "Stay in your seat, Horace," he commanded. "I have good news, but I do not want you to become too excited. Your Elsie is awake, and she appears to have passed through the crisis."

The expression on Horace's drawn face mingled surprise and dread. "What?" he managed to say.

"She is alive, my friend, but not out of the woods entirely. Her hold on life is still quite fragile, but the fever is gone, and she has survived the night. I am at last hopeful that she will recover."

Horace rose from his seat and was reaching for his jacket when the doctor stopped him. "No, Horace, you cannot see her now. We cannot risk another relapse, and I am not altogether sure she knows you yet. Until she asks for you, I must insist that you stay apart from her. Difficult as this is, I know you will do nothing to jeopardize her recovery."

"Has she spoken at all?" Horace asked, trying to take in the whole of the doctor's statements.

"Yes," the doctor replied, "but only to ask for her Bible."

Horace reached to his table and took up the little book. Handing it to the physician, he said in a near-whisper, "It has saved us both, I believe with all my heart. Please, return it to her."

With the worn volume in his hand, the doctor departed to return to the sickroom, and Horace, shaking with the shock of the news, fell to his knees and poured forth his thanksgiving for Elsie's life. Then and there, he consecrated himself, with all his talents and possessions, to the service of God who had shown such mercy in restoring the light to his life.

Elsie progressed slowly during the next few days. Although everyone in the household rejoiced at her survival, they were equally united in their concern for her safe recovery. But she soon gained enough strength to speak and ask questions. Mrs. Travilla, Adelaide, and Chloe continued their constant vigil, attending to Elsie's every need. Edward Travilla, who had assumed management of Roselands as well as his own plantation throughout the period of Elsie's illness, was allowed a brief visit; though pained by her weakness, he was delighted to receive a warm smile, and he promised to visit again in the near future. (In truth, Edward had spent most of his nights at Roselands, tending to business and from the background, watching over his friend Horace.) Doctor Barton came and went several times each day and at last pronounced himself convinced that Elsie's illness had run its course.

Strangely, however, as her strength returned, Elsie asked nothing about her father. Adelaide was the first to notice the omission, and she questioned Doctor Barton. The doctor assured her that this silence on the subject of Horace was no matter for concern. But he was adamant that the father should not see the child until asked for.

The next day, Adelaide was sitting with Elsie when the little girl asked, "Have you heard from Miss Allison? She was so kind to me, and I miss her."

"I had a letter just before you became ill, dear, and she sent you her love and best wishes."

"And my Papa? Has my Papa written?"

Cautiously, Adelaide replied, "A letter came just before your illness."

"Did he say when he will return to America?" Elsie asked eagerly. "Do you think he will ever come home from Europe?"

Shaken by Elsie's apparent loss of memory, Adelaide nevertheless answered with a steady voice, "I think he will come home very soon, dearest. I know he wants to see you because his letters are full of affection for you."

"Oh, I do hope he will love me," Elsie sighed.

"He will, I am positive. Now you go to sleep," Adelaide encouraged. "We can talk of all this when you are not so tired."

Without another word, Elsie closed her eyes and drifted into a sweet sleep. When Chloe came to take over the watch, Adelaide went immediately to Horace's room to tell him what had occurred.

Horace was deeply disturbed, fearing that the fever had cost his child her reason or that the delirium had returned. Adelaide sought to assure him, saying that Elsie was looking much better and conversing quite reasonably, but she too was worried. Doctor Barton made a happier diagnosis when he heard Adelaide's story. "She is *not* losing her mind,"

213

he said firmly. "This memory failure is hardly unexpected given the seriousness of her illness and the severe emotional stress she has endured. Let's see. She remembers Miss Allison's visit but not Horace's return. That means she has lost about a year and a half of memories," he calculated. "As she heals in body and mind, I believe it quite likely that she will recover completely what she has forgotten."

Horace was enormously relieved by this prognosis and even more by the doctor's next words.

"This does change your position, Horace," Doctor Barton said with a wry smile. "At the moment, Elsie remembers nothing of your return. So you can go to her just as soon as Miss Adelaide has prepared her for your arrival."

The reunion was accomplished the following morning. To Elsie, for whom this meeting was seemingly unique, the sight of the tall, handsome man with the fashionable beard and beautiful eyes brought on none of the trembling and fear of their real first encounter.

His eyes brimming with tears, Horace gently approached Elsie's bed and took his child in his arms. Kissing her forehead and cheeks, he crooned, "My precious daughter. My precious Elsie. We will never be separated again."

"Oh, Papa," Elsie whispered happily, "I think you do love me a little."

"I love you with all my heart," he replied, softly ruffling her limp curls and kissing her again. "I love you better than life itself."

Laying her head against his shoulder, Elsie felt completely happy and very tired. As her father's cool hand gently stroked her hair, her eyelids fluttered. As she slipped into sleep, she said, "And I love my Papa. Very, very much."

From that moment, Horace took on the role of Elsie's chief caretaker. Mrs. Travilla at last felt she could return to her own home, and both Adelaide and Chloe were able to rest after their long ordeal. There was nothing Horace did not do for his child: coaxing her to eat, administering her medicines, entertaining her with his stories of Europe, reading to her — especially the Bible stories she so loved — and holding her hour upon hour in his loving embrace. He hardly left her side, and when he did, he entrusted her care only to Adelaide or Chloe. Each day, Elsie seemed to be getting a little better. She was gaining back a little of the weight she had lost; the dark shadows were fading from her eyes; she could stay awake for longer periods. But there was still no sign of her memory coming back, and underneath his joy in her physical recovery, Horace worried constantly that her mind may have been permanently affected.

One day a week or so after his 'return,' Horace was reading to Elsie when he looked up and noticed a troubled expression on her face.

"What is it, dear," he asked anxiously.

"I'm not sure, Papa," she said slowly. "I just have this feeling that I have seen you before. I mean, before you came back from Europe. Did I dream that you gave me a beautiful doll once?" She hesitated, and her look of doubt deepened. "Were you ever angry with me, Papa?"

Horace struggled to speak in cheery tones. "Don't try to think, Daughter. How could I be angry with you when I love you so dearly?"

215

He fluffed her pillow and settled her back on the bed. "Now don't vex yourself with questions."

But for the remainder of the day, Elsie remained troubled, and Horace frequently caught her looking at him with doubt in her eyes. The next morning when he came to her room, he immediately noticed her red-rimmed eyes and trembling hands.

"What ails you, little one?" he asked in fear that the sickness was returning. "Have you been crying? Do you feel ill?"

Elsie looked at him with undisguised terror in her eyes and blurted out, "I remember, Papa. I remember it all! Are you still angry with me? Are you here to send me away?"

Horace quickly engulfed her in his arms, feeling that she was trembling violently.

"Oh, no, my child! I am here for you as long as there is breath in me. I will never send you away. I have been a cruel father to you, Elsie, and shameless in the exercise of my authority. But I will never again require you to do anything that is contrary to God's teachings. Will you forgive me, dearest, for all I have made you suffer?"

Elsie was astonished. She could say only, "But it was your right to command me."

"No! I had no right to ask you to disobey God. I have learned a great deal, dear child. I have learned that I do not own you. You belong first to the Lord, and He has lent you to me for awhile. And I will one day have to give an account of my stewardship."

Horace paused to catch his breath, and then went on, "God has answered your prayers for me. I have learned to know and love Jesus as you do, and I have dedicated my life to His service. We are now traveling on the same road, my Daughter."

A New Beginning

Elsie was too overjoyed to speak. She rested her head on his shoulder, crying soft tears of happiness, and for some time, neither father nor daughter said anything. Then Horace reached for the little Bible beside Elsie's bed and asked, "May I read to you? I have come to love this book almost as well as you do. I would very much like for us to read it together as you and Miss Allison have done."

Elsie chose a passage, and Horace read. For almost an hour, they shared in God's Word. And when Horace saw that his child was growing tired, he closed the little book and knelt beside the bed to pray for them both. He thanked God for sparing Elsie and saving both their lives. He asked for grace and wisdom to guide him as he raised his child. He confessed his own failings and prayed for the strength to never again wander from God's narrow path. And he concluded by offering thanks again that he and his daughter could now walk that path hand-in-hand.

When he had said "Amen," Horace looked up into Elsie's face. She was as beautiful as he had ever beheld her. Though still thin and pale, her face was infused with the light of joy.

This had been the happiest hour of Elsie's life. For the first time, she knew in her heart that her father's love for her was every bit as deep and strong as hers for him. Whatever trials they might face in the days to come, together, father and daughter would travel the same road now, secure in the ultimate love of their God and Savior.

"I am so happy, Papa," she said, snuggling sleepily against his sheltering arm, "so very, very happy."